MIND-
SWAPPING
MADNESS

First published in 2018 by Write Laugh
12 King Street, Rotorua, 3010, New Zealand

Text © Tom E. Moffatt, 2018

Illustrations © Write Laugh, 2018

www.tomemoffatt.com

ISBN 978-0-473-42485-5 (print)
ISBN 978-0-473-42908-9 (ebook)

A catalogue record for this book is available from the National
Library of New Zealand.

Cover design and illustrations: Paul Beavis
Developmental and copy editing: Anna Bowles
Proof reading: Marj Griffiths, Rainbow Resolutions
Print book and ebook design: Smartwork Creative,
www.smartworkcreative.co.nz

This book was funded in part by Rotorua Civic Arts Trust.
For more information visit: www.rotoruacivicartstrust.org.nz/

MIND-
SWAPPING
MADNESS

Written by Tom E. Moffatt

Illustrations by Paul Beavis

For Anabella, the first episode of my favourite trilogy

Bonkers Short Stories

STORY ONE

"Buzz off, would ya?" I said, as Charlie swung his new fly swat between my face and my homework book. The stupid thing was bigger than a tennis racket and gave off a swishing-humming sound, like a lightsaber. "I've gotta learn my spellings."

I tried to focus on spelling the word 'hindrance' ... ending with 'r-a-n-C-e', not an 'S', but my brother doesn't like to be ignored.

"This is the SuperSwat, the most powerful fly swat ever made," Charlie said, waving its mesh head in front of my face again. He'd spent a whole month's pocket money on batteries just to power the thing. "It says here that it kills all insects, including bees, hornets and dragonflies." He squinted as he read from the label on the handle. "Not suitable for children," he added, looking up at me. "Which is a shame, cos otherwise I could've swatted you too!" He threw his head back in a forced laugh, as if he had just said the funniest thing ever.

BEES

HORNETS

DRAGONFLIES

At that moment an unsuspecting fly flew in through the open window, taking Charlie's attention away from me. It was only small and wasn't doing any harm, but Charlie instantly froze, like a hunter who had just spotted a trophy stag. He tiptoed across the room, holding the fly swat behind his head as if it actually were a tennis racket.

I tried to focus on spelling the word 'disappear' – one 'S', two 'P's – but it wasn't as interesting as watching Charlie test out his new weapon.

The fly rested on the wall for a few seconds and Charlie stood poised, waiting for it to take flight. As soon as it took off he swung the SuperSwat in a wide arc. When the mesh connected with the fly there was a flash of light, like a lightning bolt, and a crack so loud that I threw my pencil across the room in shock. It bounced along the carpet and rolled underneath the couch.

I didn't see what happened to the fly. There was no dead body. Nothing. It was as if it had been cremated in mid-air.

"This is so awesome!" said Charlie, grinning that squinty-eyed grin that gives him a dimple on each cheek. 'Awesome' was not the word I would have chosen. 'Destructive' maybe. Or even 'L-E-T-H-A-L' … 'lethal'. But definitely not 'awesome'.

A bigger fly took flight and shot to the far side of the room, as though terrified by what it had witnessed. Charlie prowled after it, waiting for it to land, but this fly didn't even stop for a rest. It rocketed around the room in a random pattern, leaving Charlie swinging at thin air.

At one point it flew over me, and Charlie swung the swat above my head. The humming sound was deafening and the electricity made my hair stand on end. I ducked out of the way

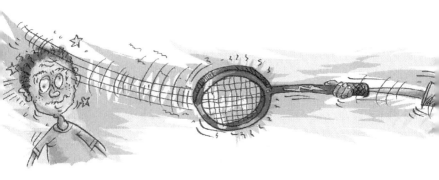

and considered taking my spellings up to my room. This was getting too dangerous.

Just then the fly dive-bombed me. Before I even raised my hands it had landed on my cheek. I lifted my arm to wave it away but Charlie was even quicker than me. He swung the swat towards my face at full speed, as if trying to knock my head off. I didn't even have time to duck as the SuperSwat's hum filled my ears.

The poor fly didn't stand a chance.

And neither did I.

White light filled my eyes and my brain sizzled, as though it had been dropped into a frying pan.

When my vision returned everything looked huge and distorted. For a second I thought I was lying on the floor with a ginormous Charlie standing over me, but the angle was all wrong. The head of the fly swat was now the size of a football pitch and as Charlie pulled it back for another swing his movements were in slow motion.

What had just happened? I knew I'd been zapped, but why was Charlie so big and slow? With the SuperSwat descending upon me I didn't have time to figure out what was going on. I leapt out of the way and the ceiling rushed towards me, my head filling with a high-pitched buzzing sound. But I didn't come back down. All of a sudden I was hovering in mid-air, watching the scene from above.

It was as though I were having an out-of-body experience. But I still had a body. I could wiggle my legs and my wings were flapping. I had wings! I could speed them up and slow them down. As if I was a fly.

Hang on a second…

I *actually* was a fly!

Down below, Charlie hit me in the face with the SuperSwat again and my arms and legs convulsed. But it wasn't me, was it? I was up high, looking down on the action. It was my body. My face was contorted and my eyes stared in opposite directions. A strange gurgling sound came from my throat, like I was drowning and being strangled at the same time. Charlie's enormous features froze and if I didn't know my brother better I'd say he looked concerned.

"George?" he said. "Are you all right?"

I tried to tell him what an idiot he was but no noise came out.

The other me, or George, didn't say anything either. He just vomited on my spelling book. A big splodge of yellowy mush covered up my weekly words and my heart froze. How would I explain *that* to Mrs Buhari?

My body slumped off the chair and hit the ground with a thud. Bits of saliva and vomit dribbled from my mouth as my arms flapped lamely on the carpet. On second thoughts, my spelling book wasn't my biggest concern.

I looked at myself lying on the floor, arms flapping as if I was trying to fly.

Then it hit me.

I must have swapped bodies with the fly. The fly was trapped in my body and I was up here, buzzing around the room. How crazy was that?

"Stop mucking around, George," my brother said, his voice high-pitched and wavering. "I didn't hit you that hard!"

He'd thrown the SuperSwat onto the couch and was waving his hands in front of my face, as though checking to see if anyone was home. I wasn't surprised that there was panic in his voice. My own face was looking utterly bonkers.

I took my eyes off the two giant humans and looked around the room for the first time. It was an incredible sight! The floor stretched out below me for what seemed like miles. It was as though the wall on the far side of the living room was three or four blocks away. And the ceiling was so high it was practically like being outside.

I leaned forwards, revved my wings and was suddenly whizzing around the room, dodging the pale-green lightshade that hung down like an enormous circus tent.

Charlie was bent over my body, gripping my jumper and trying to shake some life into me. I flew down for a closer look, loving the wind in my face as I buzzed around my stupid giant-sized brother.

When Charlie spotted me, his expression changed.

"You!" he said, actually talking to a fly. "This is all your fault!"

He left his little brother dribbling on the floor and picked the SuperSwat up off the couch. But his movements were still in slow motion. I'd already done two laps of the room by the time he'd turned the SuperSwat back on. This was going to be easy.

I watched him come towards me, his nastiest dimple-grin plastered over his face. He swung the fly swat slowly in my direction. All I had to do was swivel my body and I sped to the right, riding on the gust of wind caused by the swat. It missed me by a mile.

"You're gonna die for what you did to my brother!"

I couldn't believe Charlie was blaming the fly. It was him who hit me in the face. The fly was just an innocent bystander. Or was it a by-flyer? Anyway, that annoyed me so much. When would my stupid brother start taking responsibility for his own actions?

He leapt across the room and took another swing. Panic rose up inside my tiny body. He was still super-slow but that swat was huge. It was like trying to dodge a falling skyscraper. It came right for me and I had to rev my wings at full speed to get out of the way. I rode the air-wave over to the wall above the couch and stayed close to the ceiling, weaving in and out of the thick grey cobwebs that were hanging down like vines. The tops of the picture frames looked like dusty landing strips below me as I did a lap of the room, trying to stay as far away from the SuperSwat as I could.

But Charlie wouldn't give up that easily. He jumped up onto the couch and took another swing at me. It wasn't as close as before, but it still had me very worried. If he even clipped me with that thing I would be toast. And my body would be stuck with fly brains for the rest of its life. They would probably lock it up in some loony bin and throw away the key.

I stuck close to the walls and ceiling, doing several more laps of the living room. It was amazing how big and different everything looked from up here. The vases on the mantelpiece

looked like deep, dark caves and there was a layer of dust on almost everything. In one corner there was a spider with huge pincers, staring at me with its eight eyes. Its body wasn't much bigger than mine but its legs were like eight long lampposts and it was surrounded by a mass of webs. I made sure I didn't go too close to that corner.

Jetting around at full speed was making my wings tired. I needed to rest and come up with a plan.

It was easier to land on the ceiling than I thought it would be. I could barely feel any gravity at all, so it was almost like coming into land on the ground. The only problem was finding a clean landing site. There were large brown piles of poo scattered all over the place, as if a herd of cows had been grazing on the ceiling. Although somehow that didn't seem likely. Perhaps it was other flies that had done all the pooing? I found it hard to believe that I hadn't noticed so much poo before, but I guess I rarely look up at the ceiling. As soon as I found a clean area I spun around and stretched my six legs out. They gripped onto the ceiling like they were coated in glue.

From this vantage point I could see myself wriggling around on the floor. Fly-brained George had stopped flapping his arms now and

was trying to crawl towards the window, but he wasn't having much success. At least he wasn't going to escape in a hurry. That much I could be grateful for.

But how was I going to get back to normal? If the zap from the SuperSwat switched our minds over then I needed to land on myself and let Charlie swat us both again in the hope that we'd switch back. But with Charlie swinging that lethal weapon around, that was easier said than done. There was every chance I'd be exterminated before I got anywhere near my own body.

Charlie was busy carrying a chair across the room. He positioned it directly below me and leapt onto it, brandishing his weapon. This was not good. I saw what had happened to the first fly he'd waited for like this. It didn't stand a chance. But flies are clearly not that bright. Just look at Fly-brained George, who right now was trying his hardest to lick his own nose. All

I had to do was outsmart my brother, which wasn't exactly hard.

I would need to stay close to the ceiling instead of flying out in the open. That way I'd be out of reach and if he did try to swipe me he would hit the ceiling.

I threw myself forwards, loving the feeling of revving my wings up and whizzing along. I stayed upside down with my feet so close to the ceiling I had to dodge some of the larger piles of poo.

Charlie took a swing with the SuperSwat but he missed me by what would have been about twenty metres in human terms. As I came to the corner of the room I twisted my body and swooped around for another lap of the ceiling, making sure I didn't get too close to the enormous spider and its web.

I knew I would need to make the dive towards my body but I wanted to mentally prepare myself first. And now I was doing my low-flying on the ceiling I didn't have to worry about being swatted.

I spun around so I was facing down and my wings were almost tapping the ceiling, just in time to see the mesh grid of the SuperSwat heading straight for me. This time there was no escape. I only had time to brace myself for certain death. I could feel the rushing wind and the buzz of electricity in the air as the swat got within two or three wingspans of me. There was an almighty crunch and I stopped flapping my wings, reluctantly embracing death.

Death felt like falling.

Hang on.

I …

was …

falling …

I flapped my wings and the falling became flying again.

Why wasn't I dead? If that thing had hit me there was no way I could have survived. Maybe the sound I had heard had been the SuperSwat hitting the ceiling?

"You stupid little pest," my brother's voice boomed. "I'm going to get you if it's the last thing I do!"

I had never seen Charlie so determined. There were big beads of sweat on his enormous forehead and his face was bright red. He rushed after me so fast that even in slow motion it was quite daunting. He actually leapt over the dribbling version of me to get to the flying me. This was so weird.

He wasn't standing on a chair now, so I soared upwards again until I had the height advantage.

I needed to stay up high enough to be safe, but where he would still think he could reach me. I wanted him to have another swing.

Sure enough he swung the enormous SuperSwat at me, but I judged it well. I twisted my body and rode the air currents until I was out of reach.

This was my chance. As soon as the head of the swat passed me I plummeted downwards. Charlie changed direction and came after me, but it felt like I had enough time. I was going to make it.

Fly-brained George was still lying on his side, seemingly trying to V-O-M-I-T onto the carpet. Fortunately my stomach was now empty, so all he could do was retch and dribble.

I could sense Charlie behind me as I swooped down. But I was so close now. Fly-brained George's head loomed up in front of me like an enormous rock formation and I came in to land on a field of hair. There was an ear about three blocks away and it was so strange to think that that huge flappy thing was actually part of me.

I didn't have time for any more weird thoughts. The swat was bearing down on me and there was absolutely no escaping it this time. I tucked my legs and wings in as

tight as they would go, trying to make myself as small as possible.

I braced myself for the static buzz and bright white light.

But they didn't come.

Instead one of the metal wires of the SuperSwat's grid crashed into me like a locomotive.

BOOM!

My wings folded over my face and my legs got tangled up in each other. Wind rushed by me and then I crashed into something else. Something soft.

Only three of my eyes would open and my vision was blurry and grey.

Carpet. I was face down on the carpet.

But why hadn't we switched back? Charlie had successfully hit me with the SuperSwat, so I should be either back in my own body or dead.

"Why the heck are you not working?" Charlie's voice boomed. I flapped my wings to turn myself over and peeled my two remaining eyes open. As the room came into focus I could see him fiddling with the long handle of the swat, trying to get the batteries out. Oh no. It must have broken when it hit the ceiling.

Please don't let it be permanently damaged. That stupid thing was my only hope of getting myself back to normal.

I tried to walk along the tufts of carpet while Charlie was fixing his SuperSwat, but all six of my legs were shaking too hard. They kept getting tangled up in each other and I'd fall over and end up in one of the gullies. My wings felt like they were made of cardboard, but after fluttering them for a few seconds they began to flap normally.

I could do this. I had to do this.

I stood up and buzzed my wings while trying to run forwards. My legs got entangled and I bounced along the carpet, at least getting myself a little closer to my target.

Charlie said, "Yes!" and his voice was accompanied by the deathly buzz of the SuperSwat. "Now you're dead meat, you stupid little fly!"

He stepped towards me, brandishing the swat like a hockey stick. I was less than a metre away from my own face, but it felt like the entire length of our school playground.

I revved my wings again and this time was able to half-fly, half-run.

But Charlie was sweeping the swat along the floor towards me. There would be no escaping it this time. I had to make contact with Fly-brained George. But would that even be enough? If it wasn't, then I would be killed and F-B-G would get nothing more than another nasty shock.

It felt like too much of a gamble. But what choice did I have? The swat's mesh was approaching like a metal tsunami. I sped up, my wings flapping more freely now.

I was almost there.

The face was right ahead of me, about the same distance away as the swat at my rear.

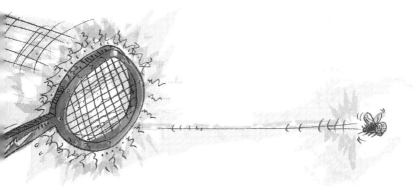

I aimed for the nose, since it was a little bit closer. I reached out with my front legs and touched down on the tip. The buzz behind me was deafening and felt like it was pulling at me, sucking me in.

Any second now.

Then I had an idea. Below me was a dark opening, like a cave. It was exactly the right size to protect me, just in case my plan didn't work.

I ducked inside the cave as the electricity buzzed all around me.

A crack filled my brain and it felt like I had just been struck by lightning. The whole world went white and the pain was unbearable, like my entire head had been deep-fried.

I opened my eyes to see my brother's evil grin staring down at me.

"Gotcha!"

"Ow!" I said. "That really hurt!"

"George? You're okay?"

I was about to call him a very rude name when I realised that there was a fly up my nose.

"Ewwww!" I said. I blocked the other nostril and snorted, sending the fly shooting out and bouncing along the floor.

Before I could stop him, Charlie stretched out his foot and squished the fly into the carpet, twisting his heel to make sure it was dead.

My mouth dropped open.

"What did you do that for?" I shouted, unable to believe he'd actually killed that poor fly.

Charlie just squinted at me and raised one of his shoulders, as though he'd done absolutely nothing wrong.

I snatched the SuperSwat out of his hand and swung it back above my head.

"I'm going to make you pay for that!" I said.

He turned to run but I managed to swing the fly swat and catch him right on the bum. There was a loud crack and he leapt into the air, clutching a bum cheek in each hand.

I drew back for another swing but Charlie was already high-tailing it out of the room. Instead of following him I looked up at the corners of the ceiling. Where was that spider? If I could swat them both at the same time that would really teach Charlie a lesson.

STORY TWO

A fly buzzes right in front of my face. I open my mouth and my tongue shoots out almost automatically, plucking it from mid-air.

It's still buzzing as it slips down my throat.

Yuck!

Flies aren't normally too bad, but this one tastes like poo. Actual poo.

It was probably crawling all over a fresh one only moments ago. It's so disgusting.

I was on my way to check out some of the main camping spots, but I think I'll head to the river to eat some mosquitoes

ACTUAL
P O O

instead. That'll fill my tummy and get rid of this nasty taste at the same time. And it's not like there's ever anyone camping at this time of year anyway.

I shuffle around so I'm facing towards the river and peer through a gap in the ferns.

Wait a second.

Is that light up ahead? No, it can't be. It's too far from the usual spots. It must be moonlight

reflecting off a broken bottle or something. I scurry forwards, knocking fern leaves and small twigs aside. I need to get a better look, just in case. There's an old tree stump to my left, so I turn towards it and keep moving forwards, one leg at a time. It's easier to walk than hop. It takes less energy and I can go much further in a night.

When I get to the base of the stump I lean back and kick off with my hind legs. I briefly fly though the air then land on the stump with a thud, knocking the wind out of me. When the pain subsides I turn to my right.

Fire!

There is fire over there!

And it's only a small one. It must be my first hunters of the year!

The fluttery feeling of hope fills my stomach. Or it could be that poo-flavoured fly I just ate.

No, it's definitely hope. This is going to be the year that someone finally kisses me. I can feel it in my toady bones.

It won't be these guys. No way. You only get tough hunters out at this time of year. Not the 'oh-there's-a-cute-toad-I-think-I'm-going-to-kiss-it' kind. But at least this will give me some practice. I can hide in the undergrowth and scope them out. If I'm lucky they'll have a conversation about what's been going on in the world. And they might even leave a few scraps of food around. Real food.

My stomach rumbles at the thought of it.

I hop down from the stump and move towards the flames, being careful to keep my noise down. I don't want them to hear me coming. The shadows are flickering all around me now and I can hear the crackle of the fire. I place one foot in front of the other, keeping to the trees and creeping slowly forwards.

"Oh no, mine's caught fire!" a high-pitched voice shrieks.

A child! There is a child here. At this time of year. My little heart speeds up and my body trembles.

"Just blow it out," says a woman's voice, "and be careful not to burn yourself. It'll be really hot."

My mouth drops open and I let out a small involuntary croak.

That sounded just like my mum. But it couldn't be? Could it? After all these years?

I slowly approach, using a tree for cover. Then, when I'm right behind the tree, I peer around the edge of the trunk.

There are just the two of them. A woman and a young girl. They're sitting on camping chairs beside the fire, roasting marshmallows on sticks. Behind them I can see the domey silhouette of a tent.

It's hard to make out their faces in the dim glow of the fire, but I can see their outlines. It's not Mum. This lady's older and fatter than Mum.

And her hair is way too long. Not to mention the fact that she has a daughter who looks about nine or ten years old. Roughly my age. Or at least the age I was when I got myself stuck in this body.

The girl blows at the charred lump on the end of her stick and then slowly wraps her lips around it.

"Mmmm, it's delicious," she says through a mouthful of marshmallow.

My tummy rumbles at the thought of it. But I need to think bigger. There is a child here. If I could just get her to kiss me I'd be able to eat food like that every day. I'd never have to eat flies again.

The lady blows on her marshmallow and pops it into her mouth in one go.

"That hit the target!" she says and I let out a croak so loud that it sounds like one of Brian's burps.

That's what Mum always says!

"What was that noise?" The girl looks in my direction. But there's no way she'll see me. Not in this light, with my camouflage.

"It's probably just a frog," the woman says and her voice is so familiar it cuts through me like a knife.

It *is* my mum!

My head spins as the realisation sinks in. If I didn't have four legs I would probably fall over.

"Or it could be a toad," Mum adds wistfully. "We used to … see a toad here … all the time …" Her voice trails off as though she's lost in thought.

She's thinking about me. The real me. I know she is. And I can remember the first time the toad found us as though it were yesterday.

It was one of our first hunting trips. The evening hunt had been enjoyable but we hadn't seen any deer yet. Then we'd come back to our camp and lit a fire, just like this one, and roasted marshmallows. Just me and my mum. The next morning, as I was sitting in my camping chair brushing my teeth, a big warty toad shuffled into the clearing. It walked straight up to me and sat down next to my foot, looking up at me. Mum was washing in the stream at the time.

I've since realised that the toad had been watching us all night, waiting for the right moment to approach. Just like I have done so many times since.

As I stared at it the toad did a back flip, landing perfectly on its four feet. Even now I'm impressed by that move. I've tried it hundreds of times and I usually land on my head or my back. And if I do happen to land on my feet it's anything but graceful. I can only assume the person who was stuck in this body before me was a bit of an acrobat.

Anyway, all those years ago, I was suitably impressed. The toad knew it and put on a show for me. It spun around, jumped over things, did somersaults. It really was incredible to watch a large, warty toad doing all those cool tricks.

But as soon as we heard Mum's footsteps approaching, the toad did its biggest jump yet, straight into my lap.

"I see you've made yourself a new friend," Mum said, as she sat down in the seat next to me, drying her hair with a towel.

"Look at some of the tricks it can do, Mum," I said, placing it on the ground again.

But the toad just sat there, looking up at Mum, and let out a loud croak.

"I'm not sure you're ready to join the circus quite yet," Mum said to it with a smile. "But if you keep practising, you never know."

"But … just a minute ago, it was jumping all over the place. Doing back flips. I swear."

"Perhaps it's scared of your big bad mummy!" she said, growling at us. She totally didn't believe me. And I don't blame her really. Whenever Mum was around the toad just stuck by me, like a guard-toad. But as soon as Mum popped off to do something, he would come to life, performing tricks and entertaining me in any way he could. I named him Tricky and he soon became the highlight of my hunting trips.

At first I was amazed by how he always found us. As long as we came to this region, it didn't seem to matter where we camped, he would always turn up.

"Here's your friend again," Mum would say, all slanted eyebrows and crinkly forehead. But she eventually got used to him.

Tricky started off waiting until morning to approach us, but by the third or fourth trip he would shuffle out into our clearing in the evening, usually not long after we'd lit the fire. He'd sit beside me, keeping me company and begging for scraps of food. It got to the point where I started begging Mum to go on

a hunting trip, just so that I could see Tricky.
I also begged her to let me take Tricky home,
to keep him as a pet. But Mum would never
budge, so I pestered her into taking me hunting
again. I didn't suspect a thing. I just thought it
was an ordinary toad. Special, obviously, and
super-cool, but ordinary just the same.

And then it happened.

That stupid kiss. How could I have been such
an idiot?

Brian had said Mum was crazy going hunting
so close to her due date, but Mum insisted we
squeeze in one last trip. She said that
she wanted some quality time
with me before the baby came
along, and anyway, none
of the other hunters we
met let a big stomach
stop them from
hunting. I was just
glad that I'd get to
see Tricky one last
time. Tricky must

have known we wouldn't be back for a while too, since he gave me his very best performance every time Mum turned her back. It was like he'd been practising. Triple somersaults, cartwheels, the whole works.

We'd packed up our tent, dressed the deer down and loaded the meat into our packs. I tried to take as much as I could to help Mum out. She was already carrying enough weight in her tummy. We were just about to trek back to the car; Mum had already walked ahead and I had Tricky in my hands, looking up and croaking at me.

"Bye, Tricky," I said. "Take care over winter. I'm really going to miss you." If I'd known those were the last words I'd ever say I would have said something a little more profound.

I glanced over my shoulder to make sure Mum wasn't looking, then I leaned over and kissed Tricky on the top of the head.

It happened instantly. No pain. No flash of light.

One second I was kissing. The next I was being kissed.

My own enormous face was right there in front of me, all wide eyes and huge smile.

"Yes, yes, yes! Thank you, kid," my own voice said. "Thank you so much."

I was paralysed with fear as he placed me on the ground and patted his body down – *my* body – as though checking it worked properly.

"Ha!" he said, squeezing my mouth into a sly smile as he looked down at me. "That old hag said I'd never find someone kind enough to kiss me. But I didn't need kind, did I? I just needed a stupid kid. And that's you, Ari! Sorry, why am I calling *you* Ari? That's my name now!"

And with that he began to walk away.

I was panicking so much I could barely breathe. The whole world looked so different. So big and scary. I shouted at him to stop, to give me my body back. But all that came out was a series of loud croaks.

He'd only walked about ten metres when he stopped and turned around, but it felt like hundreds of metres from my new perspective. "Just find some high ground and dig yourself a deep hole. You'll sleep through winter," he said. Then he rummaged in the side pocket of my bag and pulled out a packet of chicken-flavoured potato chips that I'd been saving for the ride home. He opened the bag and dropped it on the ground by his feet, spilling a few chips onto the dirt.

Mum stopped walking and turned around. "Come on, Ari," she called. "If you take much longer this baby's going to be born in the forest!"

My body turned and walked off, without even glancing back over his shoulder.

That must be ten years ago now. And that impostor has been in my body for the whole time. He must have convinced my mum to go hunting elsewhere. Or maybe they stopped hunting altogether.

Until now.

I can't believe it. My mum is right there in front of me, gently waving her marshmallow over the flames. With my sister. My actual sister. Who was just a bump in Mum's tummy last time I saw her. I am so excited I have to clench every muscle in my body to stop myself from croaking. I don't want to draw attention to myself. I have to come up with some sort of a plan.

I nestle down between two roots of a tree, keeping still so that no birds or possums see me. Then I listen.

This is what I do whenever I find hunters in the forest. I sit, with my eyes closed, and listen to their conversations. And for a few short moments every month or two, my life feels normal. Like I'm still human. But this time is even better. It feels like I'm back on a hunting trip with my mum. Listening to her tell hunting stories.

"If we can't carry it out between you and me, then we're not going to shoot it. One time we shot two stags, both beauties, they were." I give a big toady smile as I hear her tell this story. I was only eight or nine at the time, but I can remember it as if it were yesterday. "We dressed one of them, but even that nearly had too much meat for Ari and I to carry, so we filled our backpacks and left a whole stag propped against a tree. But by the time we got back to it the next morning there was just a pile of skin and bones. The wild pigs had stripped it clean."

At some point I drift off to sleep, the sound of my mum's and sister's voices soothing me like a lullaby.

I wake up the next morning to chirpy birds, as always. But this time it's different. It's like music to my ears and it makes me want to dance and sing. Or at least croak. Mum and my sister are tiptoeing around in the dark, getting ready for their morning hunt. Mum whispers the same instructions that she used to give me before we left camp each morning.

"Make sure your laces are tight."

"Tia, have you got your water bottle?"

"Don't touch your rifle unless I'm right beside you!"

And then they're off, disappearing into the darkness before first light breaks through the trees. I wish I could go with them. With my mum and baby sister, Tia. But there are other things on my mind right now. Firstly, I am starving hungry. All I ate yesterday were a few measly flies and a couple of beetles, and the thought of some proper food has my stomach virtually croaking.

LACES

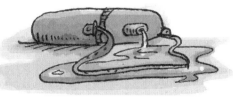

WATER

RIFLE

I step out into the clearing and look around. The tent is all zipped up and there's a blackened circle at the centre of the camp. Everything else has been put neatly away, including the chairs. Mum likes to leave her campsite as tidy and natural as possible.

I shuffle over to the edge of the fire, my eyes searching the ground where my sister was sitting. There's a black lump that looks like a piece of charcoal, but as I approach I see pink cracks running along its surface and I let out an excited croak.

Marshmallow.

It's an entire marshmallow.

It must have caught fire and fallen from her stick. I open my mouth wide and gobble it whole. Toads don't chew their food, but they still taste it as it slips down their throats. And this tastes like pure sugary deliciousness. It's by far the yummiest thing I have eaten in months, even with all the burnt bits and specks of dirt.

I sit for a moment, savouring the flavour in my mouth, then search for other scraps. I don't find as much as I do with other hunters, since Mum is always vigilant with her food. She keeps it in an airtight chiller in the tent, so the possums don't get at it. In the end I make do with a couple of beetles. But it's okay. I can still feel the marshmallow slowly dissolving in my stomach.

My next priority is to come up with a plan. All I know so far is that I'll have to be very careful. To my mum's eyes I am the very same toad that used to visit her and her son all those years ago. I don't know what would have happened when the impostor got home in my body, but I can only imagine that Mum and Brian noticed quite a few changes over the weeks, months and years. I wonder if she ever suspected the toad. Or blamed it in any way? I doubt that she would have, but I can't be too careful. If Mum freaks out and doesn't let me anywhere near Tia then I might never get out of this body.

The sun is high in the sky by the time I hear the sound of their approach. I'm already back in my spot behind the tree, so I just listen to them setting up the camp again and cooking bacon and eggs on the fire. The smell of bacon is almost more than my stomach can handle. So is their conversation.

"It's way easier hunting without Ari crashing through the undergrowth and moaning about cruelty to animals," Tia says at one point, the sound and smell of sizzling bacon filling the air.

"He wasn't always like that," Mum says, her voice sounding both hurt and defensive. "When Ari was about your age he was actually a pretty good hunter."

"No!" Tia says, her laugh cutting through the birdsong. "I don't believe it. He's gotta be the worst hunter ever. The only thing I've ever seen him hit is a tree. It's almost like he misses the deer on purpose."

Neither of them speak for a few moments. I sit

there, listening to the sound of the spitting pan and a tui warbling in the trees overhead, hoping that they'll say more.

"Do you miss him, Mum?" Tia asks.

It's like all the sounds in the forest stop while I wait to hear her reply.

"Yes, I do, love," she says eventually. "But I think he's gone for good now."

"You don't think he'll drop by next time the circus is in town?"

"I guess there's a chance he'll pop in for a cup of tea," Mum says, her voice high-pitched and shaky. "But your brother has become very independent. He doesn't need his mother any more. And he certainly doesn't see eye to eye with your father."

There is silence again, but this time it's filled with the sound of my own toady heartbeat.

"Don't worry, Mum," Tia says. "I'm not going anywhere!"

My stomach feels both full and empty at the same time. I can't see them but I'm pretty sure they are holding hands. Or hugging.

Tia seems really nice. But I try not to think about that. I can't. She's my only way out of this stupid body and back to my family. To *my* mother. It would be amazing if there was another way. But there just isn't.

There's nothing but small talk while they eat their breakfast. Then Mum says, "I'm going to wash the dishes in the river. You collect some firewood. But don't stray too far away. Make sure you can see the tent at all times."

I hear the sound of clattering pans, then footsteps leading away from the camp.

This is it. This is my chance to show myself.

I'm just about to leave my spot between the roots when Tia steps out from behind the tree. She bends down and picks up a branch from only a metre away from me. It's amazing, though. She could have gone in any direction but she headed straight for me.

I turn and hop away from her, just like a real toad would.

"Whoa," she says, taking a step back. "Hi there, big guy,"

I hop into the clearing and head straight for the chair Tia was sitting on. Once I'm underneath it I turn around and get my first proper look at her in daylight.

She's standing at the edge of the clearing with the branch in her hand, looking down at me. She's wearing khaki pants and a T-shirt with Bambi on it, which is pretty funny really, considering the fact that she just spent her morning hunting deer. Her fair hair is tied back in a ponytail, but strands have come loose and are blowing in the breeze. Her face is all brown eyes and crooked teeth. Even though she's got Brian's lighter skin and hair, she is still the spitting image of Mum. And me, for that matter. There's absolutely no doubt that she is my sister.

"Hey, froggy," she says, "are you hungry?"

I say, "Heck yeah!" but all that comes out is a croak.

Tia walks towards me and picks up a length of bacon rind from next to the fire. She then reaches under the chair and dangles it in front of me. I flick my tongue out and pull it into my mouth. It takes about four swallows to disappear entirely and it's the most delicious thing I have eaten in years. Even better than the marshmallow.

I croak again and move a few steps towards Tia.

"You want more, do ya, big guy?" Tia rummages around next to the fire until she finds another couple of rinds. She dangles them in front of me and I whip them in with my tongue, one at a time.

My plan is to be friendly and clever, but not to do anything too entertaining. I wouldn't be able to do anything like the tricks that impressed me so much, and anyway, I don't want Mum to freak out and keep Tia away from me.

By the time all the bacon rind and bread crusts are gone my stomach feels full to the brim. It's all aches and rumbles too, but it's worth it to have the lingering taste of real food in my mouth. I must remember to eat a few beetles or flies later though, since it's what this body is used to.

Tia continues collecting firewood, so I hop along after her and she seems pretty happy about it.

"Look, Mum, I've made a new friend," Tia says and I turn around to see our mum standing at the edge of the clearing, staring at me with her mouth wide open. Her hair is flecked with grey and she's put on a lot of weight. But there is no doubt that it's Mum.

"Tricky?" she says, still all wide eyes and gaping mouth. "I don't believe it."

"What's wrong, Mum?" Tia says, her eyebrows squished together. "It's only a frog."

"It's actually a toad," Mum says, taking a few steps towards me. "And it looks just like one your brother befriended many years ago."

"Ari befriended a toad? No way!" Tia says, shaking her head. "He hates frogs and toads. When one jumped onto the deck a few years ago he nearly had a heart attack."

"Well, he wasn't like that when he was little. He really loved that guy. He named him Tricky."

I let out a croak and hop over to Tia's foot.

"He didn't do any … umm … tricks, did he?"

Tia looks at her mum as if she has lost her marbles. "What are you talking about?"

"Oh, you know … like back flips or somersaults?"

"It's actually a toad, Mum. Not one of Ari's circus friends."

Mum looks down at me and does one of her closed-lip half-smiles that she always did when she didn't believe me. My heart nearly leaps out of my chest. I have missed her so much.

"It seems like Ari was the tricky one," she says in a soft voice, more to herself than to anyone else.

The middle part of the day was always one of my favourite times on hunting trips, and this one is no exception. I feel like I've died and gone to toad heaven. After all the chores are done Mum gets *Harry Potter and the Prisoner of Azkaban* out and they both sit in their chairs while Mum reads out loud. I hop up onto Tia's lap, close my eyes and listen to the story.

Mum's voice hasn't changed a bit and it's like I'm back in my bedroom, all those years ago, just a normal boy listening to bedtime stories.

Reading wasn't exactly my favourite thing when I was in my own body, but I've really missed it over the years. Once I found an old hunting magazine that someone left behind in the bush. I dug myself a new hole right next to it and spent every day reading, until it became so wrinkled by the rain that the words were no longer legible. But having a story read to me is something else. It makes me long to be human again. To have this every day.

In the late afternoon Mum and Tia start packing up, ready for their evening hunt. They haven't said how long they're staying, but my guess is that they'll see how they do. If they get a deer this evening they'll pack their things onto their backs and head to the car tonight. No deer and they'll stay for the morning hunt too. I used to love going to school straight from a hunting trip. It felt like our little secret. And like we'd really made the most out of the weekend.

Tia keeps glancing over at me while she's packing her things, as though she's checking I'm still here. She's biting her lip, as if there's something on her mind.

Then she stops what she's doing and turns to Mum. "Muuuum," she says, her voice as soft and sweet as a marshmallow. "Can I take Trickster home with me? Keep him as a pet?"

My heart pounds so fast it makes my throat vibrate. Imagine that! I'd be back in my own home. With my mum and Brian and Tia. I'd get to eat decent food every day. I'd be comfortable. And warm. And I'd be able to get Tia to kiss me. Surely I would. Given enough time. Then it would be like this never happened. As though all those things had never been taken from me.

I suddenly think about Tia. About how nice she is. About how great it would be if she was my sister. But it could never be. Only one of us can live with my family and surely it should be me. I'm the one who's been trapped in a toad's body for the last ten years. Living alone in the forest.

"Absolutely not," Mum says, sending my dreams crashing to the ground in flames. "You know my thoughts on conservation. We leave nothing behind and we take nothing with us."

"Except as many deer as we can carry."

"That's different, dear," Mum says. "They're a pest. We're actually helping the native wildlife by culling them. That toad lives in this forest. It's his home. We can't take him away and stick him in a cage. It wouldn't be fair."

I let out a long, loud croak to show them that I wouldn't mind at all. Honestly.

"But look at him, Mum. He loves hanging out with us. And he'd make a great pet."

"Be that as it may, you are not taking him. And that's final."

Tia continues shoving things into her backpack without saying another word.

So that's it, then.

I'm staying right here.

Who knows when they'll come hunting again? If they even will. I'll probably have to wait another ten stupid years. It's *so* unfair!

The shadows are long and my mood is dark when they head off into the forest for their evening hunt. I barely look up to see them go. I don't even head back to the safety of the tree roots. Who cares if a possum comes and eats me? It would be better than having to spend the rest of my life out here, all on my own.

I sit there, in the middle of the clearing, listening to the sounds of the forest as it comes alive for the night. Before long I drift off to sleep, even though I'm supposed to be nocturnal.

I wake up with a jerk. Two hands have just grabbed hold of me and lifted me into the air. I can't see a thing other than fingers and treetops. Who's got me? Is it Mum? Tia? Or someone else?

Next thing I know I am shoved into a dark hole. Up above I can see Tia's face looking down at me, all mischief and concern. There's the sound of a zip closing and it's suddenly pitch black. I'm in her backpack. I must be.

"You pack the tent down while I prepare this guy," Mum says, her voice muffled through the fabric of the bag.

So they shot a deer and are making their way home tonight. With me. Thank you, Tia, thank you so much.

All is still for a while, then I feel myself being hoisted up into the air and slung over Tia's shoulder.

"Have you said goodbye to Tricky?" Mum asks.

"No, I can't find him anywhere," Tia says. "He must have run away."

"Don't worry, love," Mum says. "I'm sure you'll see him next time we come hunting."

Then they start to walk back to the car. The steady up-down motion is quite soothing and I soon find myself drifting off to sleep again. I have no idea how much time passes, but before long the sounds of the forest and Mum and Tia's chatter are replaced by the drone of a car engine.

Then, all of a sudden, the zip is being undone and light pours in.

"Hi, Trickster," Tia asks, her voice a soft whisper. "How did you go?"

I give a croak and, as my eyes adjust to the brightness, look around the room. My room! Sure, it looks a bit different to what it used to. But the bed is the same. And so is the battered old bedside table. I can't believe that I am actually back in my own bedroom. After all these years. It's like a dream come true.

All I have to do is get Tia to kiss me and I'll practically have my old life back. It will be as though none of this ever happened. Almost, anyway. Being in a girl's body might take a bit of getting used to. And there is the small detail of what I would do with toad-Tia, but I'm too excited to think about that now.

Tia places me down on the middle of the bed and I can't believe how soft it is. It's incredible. I give a couple of excited hops, then I flop onto my back, close my eyes and pretend to go to sleep.

Tia lets out a laugh.

"That's it, Trickster," she says, "make yourself at home. The only problem is that we're going to have to keep you hidden from Mum and Dad."

I let out a croak-whisper to show her that that's not going to be a problem.

Then I hear footsteps outside the door. Tia's eyes bulge and she stares at me helplessly as the door starts to open.

Quick as a flash I leap towards the head of the bed, tucking my arms and

legs in. I slide along the sheet and disappear underneath the pillow, hoping that I made it before I was spotted.

"Why aren't you ready for bed, dear?" Mum's voice asks. "You know you've got school tomorrow."

"I ... just thought ... I'd unpack first," Tia says slowly. She clearly thought she was about to be busted.

I stay under the pillow until they've both left the room, then I hop down and start to explore my old bedroom. It's so warm and cosy, and it seems enormous to me in a toad's body. The carpet feels delicious under my feet as I hop around. When I've checked everything out I duck underneath the bed, which is like a dark cave, so that I won't be spotted if Mum or Brian come into the room.

A short while later I hear footsteps and the bed squeaks above me. Then I get to listen to Brian continuing with Harry Potter. At first Tia explains what Brian missed, then I get lost in the sound of Brian's voice. He's an excellent storyteller, putting on hilarious accents for all the different characters. I don't want it to end.

Eventually the lights go out and goodnight kisses are passed around.

There's no way I'll get a kiss so soon, but I decide to at least show myself. To try to establish a bedtime routine in the hope that she'll kiss me goodnight one day. I shuffle out from under the bed and let out a quiet croak.

"Oh, hi, Trickster," Tia says in a whisper. "I nearly forgot to say goodnight to you!"

She reaches over and scoops me up before laying me gently down on the bed next to her. I shuffle up and place my head on the pillow, right beside her head.

"You're so cute," Tia whispers. "I'll probably be in heaps of trouble if we get found out. But I don't care. It's their fault for not letting me get a pet. I know it was just because Ari didn't like animals, but he's gone now. And you know what? I'm pretty sure he's never coming back."

My heart almost stops as she pulls the blankets up and snuggles into me with her forehead. We are so close now, all she'd have to do is tilt her head up and she'd be able to kiss me.

Go on. Kiss me. Then Ari will come back. He'll be back for good.

"Don't tell anyone, but that's probably a good thing. He just locked himself away in his room most of the time anyway, telling me to get lost if I went anywhere near him. Plus he'd have a heart attack if he ever saw you."

There is a tight feeling in my chest, like my heart is being crushed. It's so sad that she had such a rubbish brother. If only I hadn't been so stupid and kissed the toad. I'd have loved to have Tia as a sister. I know I would have played with her and looked out for her.

Suddenly Tia looks straight at me. Her enormous face is right there, all sad eyes and puckered lips.

"Goodnight, Trickster," she says and she kisses me on the top of my head.

Then I am lying on my side in the bed with the blankets over me.

The toad is right next to me, its eyes unblinking.

She did it.

She actually kissed me!

I throw the covers off and stand up in the bed.

The toad is looking up at me, all warts and bulging eyes.

"Yes!" I shout. "She did it! I'm free! I'm actually free!"

There is the sound of heavy footsteps in the hallway.

Oops!

I quickly sit down as the door is flung open. But the toad is still in the middle of my bed.

I grab the pillow and shove it down on top of the toad just as Mum barges into the room, closely followed by Brian.

"What on earth is going on, young lady?" Mum asks.

"Jeez," says Brian, "are you all right? I thought you were having a fit."

"Sorry, Mum," I say, keeping my hand pushing firmly down on the pillow so that Tia-toad doesn't wriggle free. "Sorry, Brian. I just had the craziest dream. But it's okay, Mum and Brian. I'm here now. And I'm okay." The words won't stop pouring from my mouth. It's the first time I have spoken in years and it's like a dam just burst.

Mum and Brian glance at each other, then they come and sit next to me on the edge of the bed and put their arms around me in a three-way cuddle. It feels so good I almost start crying.

"Your *father* and I love you so much," Mum says. Oops! Of course Tia would call Brian 'Dad'.

"And we'd never let anything bad happen to you," Brian says.

My heart is glowing like the sun. This is one of the happiest moments of my life.

Then Mum says, "Yes, we'll always protect you, Tia."

I suddenly realise that this is not *my* life. It's my sister's. And she deserves it every bit as much as I do. Perhaps even more so. After all, Brian is *her* biological dad, not mine. And this is definitely her body. My body has joined the circus and will probably never come back. And even if it did, it's not really my body any more, is it? That impostor has been in it for nine or ten years, making it his own. The toad is my body now, whether I like it or not.

I suddenly realise what I have to do. I will explain what happened to Tia. I'll tell her absolutely everything. Then I'll kiss her back and she can look after me. It will still be like being part of the family. I'll get to eat all my favourite foods. And she might even let me have a go in her body on special occasions, like Christmas or my birthday. And that will be enough. It will be a hundred times better than living on my own in the forest.

I've still got one hand holding the pillow down, and Mum and Brian are still cuddling me. I don't want it to stop but I also want to talk to Tia. To explain what has happened.

"Thanks, Mum, thanks Br... Dad, I feel much better now." I give them both a big kiss on the cheek. "I love you so much!"

Mum and Brian exchange glances again, then they stand up and walk out of the room.

They're smiling as they close the door. And so am I. I want to go back in the toad's body. I want to spend the rest of my days being looked after by my awesome sister. Living with my awesome family.

"I'm so sorry, Tia," I say, as I lift up the pillow. "Let me expl..."

I stop mid-sentence.

The toad is lying completely still, its arms and legs stretched out.

It looks ...

No no no no.

It can't be. No. No!

My eyes fill up with tears and almost instantly they are rushing down my cheeks and dripping onto my pyjamas.

I wasn't pushing down that hard. But she couldn't breathe. For all that time.

I pick the toad up and it's lifeless and still in my hands.

What have I done? I've stolen my sister's body and then suffocated her. How will I ever live with myself?

My breath is coming out in big snotty gasps as I sit on the edge of the bed, the toad lying across my lap.

If only I hadn't stumbled across their camp. If only Tia had left me in the forest. Being a toad isn't all that bad. It would be better than this.

Anything would be better than this.

As I stare down at the toad, its foot twitches. Ever so slightly. But it was movement. Could it still be alive?

I suddenly know what I've got to do.

Even if it means I'm going to die.

I scoop the toad up and lift it towards my face, its fat tummy cupped in my hands. Its legs dangle down limply and its eyes look forwards unblinking. I just hope there is enough life – and magic – left for this to work.

A tear drips from the end of my nose and lands on the toad's back, trickling down its skin, getting slowly absorbed as it goes.

I pucker my lips and am just about to give the toad a big kiss on the mouth when I notice that I am standing in the middle of the forest.

I'm suddenly all disorientated.

The toad is looking up at me, all bulging eyes and warty skin. It lets out a loud croak, then does a somersault, spinning around perfectly in the air before landing back in my palms with a slap.

It's alive!

Although, why wouldn't it be?

What the heck is going on?

Mum is walking up ahead, her large backpack strapped to her back. That's right. We're hunting.

But why am I standing here?

Of course. I was about to give Tricky a goodbye kiss. He is still in my hands, staring up at me. He lets out a forceful croak, as if ordering me to kiss him.

Suddenly that doesn't feel like such a good idea. I don't know why. I just don't trust him anymore. Toads shouldn't be able to do tricks like that. And the way he always finds us, no matter where we set up camp. It's not right.

I quickly lower Tricky to the ground, placing him on the dirt between a twig and a dried leaf. As I pull my hand away he snaps his jaws at me and lets out an angry growl.

I back away from him and glance up towards Mum. She has stopped and turned to face me, her enormous tummy sticking out in front of her.

"Come on, Ari," she says. "If you take much longer this baby's going to be born in the forest!"

That's right! Mum's going to have a baby soon. I wonder if it's going to be a boy or a girl?

Tricky does a double backflip as he hops after me. But I'm more freaked out than impressed. I jog towards Mum without even looking over my shoulder, suddenly feeling like I don't ever want to see him again. Perhaps I'll ask Mum if we can go hunting somewhere else in the future.

As I catch up with Mum something doesn't feel quite right. Like I've just missed something. Or done something wrong. But it's okay. I'm with my mum now. And very soon I'm going to be a big brother.

CYBERSPACE INVADER

Yolanda's dad opened the door, squinting in the afternoon sun. His hair stuck out in clumps and he had dark rings under his eyes. But when he saw Jayne a huge smile filled his face.

"Hi, Jayne," he said. "It's *so* good to see you!"

Jayne smiled back. It had only been a few weeks since she'd last popped round. "Hi, is Yolanda in? She hasn't been out to play in a while."

"No, she hasn't," Yolanda's dad said, his smile and his shoulders drooping at the same time. "She's been too busy working on her project for this year's Invention Convention."

"Oh!" said Jayne, unable to hide her surprise. "Are you not helping her this time?"

Yolanda's dad let out a big puff of air through his nose and slowly shook his head.

"You know Yolanda," he said, staring down at his hands. "She *really* wants to win this time, so she doesn't want my help."

"I'm sure she just ..." Jayne said, her voice trailing off. She couldn't think of a good reason why Yolanda would have ditched her dad like that. Yolanda loved making stuff with him. They always tinkered away in the garage together. Okay, she was pretty upset when she only got runner-up last year. But that just seemed to make them both more determined.

Her dad beckoned for Jayne to follow him, then knocked gently on Yolanda's door. "Hi, sweetheart," he said in a soft voice, as though worried about disturbing her.

"NO, DAD!" came a sharp shout from inside. "I HAVE TOLD YOU I'M BUSY!"

"But Jayne's here to see you, love." His eyes widened and he bit his bottom lip as he waited for a response. Jayne couldn't believe Yolanda was treating her dad like that. No wonder the poor man looked so tired.

A loud tut came from the other side of the door. "Okaaaay," she said, as though she was doing Jayne a favour. "She can come in, but not for long. I'm really busy."

Yolanda opened the door by about twenty centimetres, which was just enough for Jayne to squeeze through. Yolanda's dad tried to poke his head around to look into the room, but the door was closed in his face.

Jayne suddenly felt a bit weird. Yolanda was one of her best friends, but the girl standing in front of her was acting more like a stranger. She'd barely spoken to her at school over the past few weeks, always being one of the last to

arrive and the first to leave. She'd missed all of their choir practices, which was totally unlike her. And now this.

"Hi, Yolanda," Jayne said, smiling awkwardly. "What have you been up to? I feel like I've barely seen you."

"Oh, you know, it's Invention Convention time again," Yolanda said, gesturing towards her bed.

Jayne glanced in the direction of the bed and her mouth dropped open in surprise. Her friend's bedroom, which was usually spotless, was a jumble of tools and random metal components. The bed was set up like a workbench, with rows of spanners, screwdrivers and little containers full of nuts and bolts covering the orange duvet. Piles of metal strips, cogs and levers were scattered around the carpet like molehills.

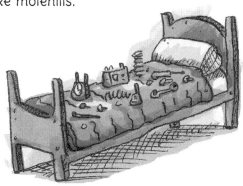

But the craziest thing was the machine that was humming and whirring away in the middle of the room.

"Whoa!" Jayne said, before she could stop herself. "What on earth is that?"

She said 'what on earth' because that thing did not look like anything from this planet. It was the strangest-looking device Jayne had ever seen. The base was only narrow but it got wider towards the top, completely defying gravity. It was nearly as tall as Jayne and there were cogs and pistons moving backwards and forwards, presumably to stop it from falling over.

"Did you make that?" Jayne asked, trying to keep the surprise out of her voice. "It's … it's … incredible!"

Yolanda smiled for the first time. "Thanks," she said, tilting her head to one side. "I've been working on it for over a month."

"Where did you get all this stuff from?" Jayne asked, making a sweeping gesture to take in all the bits and pieces that now filled Yolanda's large bedroom.

"Some of it came from around the house and the garage," she said, shifting from one foot to the other. "But I had to order quite a lot online."

"Did you build it all by yourself?" Jayne asked. The robotic hand that Yolanda and her dad made last year was pretty impressive, but Jayne had always suspected that her dad had done most of the work. Perhaps she'd been wrong.

"Sort of," Yolanda said, looking down at her feet again. "I've done all the construction myself but a friend helped me with the design."

There was definitely something fishy going on. Jayne often worked in a group with Yolanda at school and she never let anyone help with design. The only person whose ideas she would listen to was her dad, and she'd literally shut him out this time.

"Who was it?"

"No one you know."

"Who then?"

"Just someone I met online."

"Online? Like … in a chat room?"

"Yeah. One for young inventors."

"Yeah?"

"Yeah. He came up with the idea and explained how to build it."

"He?"

"Yeah, he."

"How old is *he*?"

"I don't know. He didn't say."

Jayne couldn't believe what she was hearing. After listening to Mr Brundish prattle on for hours about cyber-safety and not communicating with strangers, here was Yolanda taking instructions from some random person online. For the smartest person in their year, she was being pretty stupid.

A very nasty thought crossed Jayne's mind.

"You didn't give him your address, did you?"

Yolanda looked down at the carpet again.

"Mmm," she said quietly, "but only so he could post me some of the components I needed."

This was beginning to sound fishier than Sea World. Jayne glanced out the window to see if there were any strangers lurking around. There was a lady gardening in front of the house across the street, and a few parked cars, but nothing too out of the ordinary.

"What does it do, anyway?" Jayne asked, trying to steer the conversation in a less creepy direction.

Her efforts crashed into a brick wall.

"I'm not entirely sure," Yolanda said, raising her shoulders up to her ears.

"YOU DON'T KNOW?" Jayne asked, unable to keep the shock from her voice. "You've spent months working on this thing and you don't even know what it does?"

"Well, the theme of the convention is the Future of Communication. And he says that this will definitely win." Yolanda stared down at the carpet, clearly not wanting to make eye contact. "If we can get it working, that is."

"What do you mean? Doesn't it go?"

Yolanda shook her head, her eyes still fixed on the floor. "I've tried absolutely everything."

A ping came from her computer and she jolted to life, rushing over to read the new message. Jayne followed her and read over Yolanda's shoulder:

Where you go? Me ready for help you.

"Where's he from?" Jayne asked. "His English isn't great."

"No, he's just learning. He's from Stergak."

Stergak? Jayne had never even heard of it. Although saying that, she was pretty rubbish at geography. There were quite a few countries she'd never heard of. This one sounded like it might be in Eastern Europe.

Yolanda leaned over and typed, *I'm ready now*, into the keyboard. Then she turned and looked Jayne directly in the eyes for the first time.

"Listen, Jayne, he's going to help me fix it. But I need you to stay quiet, okay? I promised him I'd keep this a secret until we've got it working, so I don't want him to find out that you're here."

Jayne's stomach felt like a pressure cooker and all she wanted to do was rush out the door and get far away from this crazy situation. But she nodded anyway. Yolanda clearly wasn't thinking straight and someone had to look out for her.

As if to prove the point Yolanda picked up a metal bucket with circuit boards stuck to the base and a long wire dangling from it. She clipped the end of the wire to her invention, sat down on the carpet and placed the bucket over her head.

"How is that going to help?" Jayne asked. But before Yolanda could answer, the pistons and cogs started to speed up. The machine wobbled on its narrow base, its outer layer staying perfectly still while the insides spun faster and faster. The rhythmic hum intensified and Jayne's heart pounded in her chest. Was that thing even safe?

When the noise reached deafening levels Jayne ducked behind the bed, peering over the rows of tools.

An eerie green glow filled the room. Yolanda was still sitting on the floor with the metal bucket over her head. A sudden flash of green light shot out from beneath the bucket and there was a sound like a space rocket being struck by lightning in the middle of take-off. Yolanda's body jerked and then tensed up. All of a sudden the light and noise stopped, as if someone had flicked the off-switch. The cogs and pistons went back to the slow and steady rhythm that must be keeping the machine standing upright.

Yolanda poked her elbows out to her sides and grabbed hold of the metal bucket, slowly lifting it off her head. She dropped it on the floor beside her, her head jerking and jolting as she looked around the room. Then she brought her hands up to her face, studying them on both sides as though seeing them for the first time.

"Qeegag ag googah!" she said. Every hair on Jayne's body stood to attention and her stomach felt like she was on a roller coaster. That was no language Jayne had ever heard before. She didn't know what had happened to Yolanda but this was definitely not her. Sure, it was her body, but her mind had been taken over. And the way she was sitting, with her elbows pointing out and her head jutting forwards, did not look at all human.

Yolanda – or whatever it was driving her body – pushed herself up off the floor and staggered awkwardly towards the bed, as though walking for the first time. Her neck was craning forwards and her tongue was poking out of her mouth as though she was trying to taste the air.

Jayne ducked down low to keep out of sight. Her heart was thumping so loudly in her ears that she could only just hear the sound of metal objects clinking on the bed, a few centimetres above her head.

After lying there for a moment, barely daring to breathe, Jayne sneaked a peek over the edge of the bed. Yolanda was back at the machine, with a spanner clutched in each hand, tightening two bolts at once. Jayne watched in awe as her friend's body jerked around like a string puppet, tweaking and fiddling with different parts of the machine.

Eventually she flicked a red switch, that looked as though it came from an old kettle, and took a few clumsy steps backward.

The machine whirred to life, this time without any wobbling. The pistons and cogs spun but the noise was much lower and the green glow brighter. When the insides of the machine had become a blur the whole thing tipped over at a forty-five degree angle, completely defying gravity.

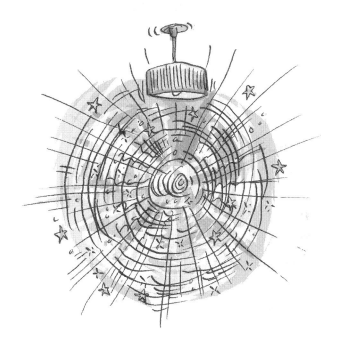

Green light poured from the top, creating a triangular screen, like the sail of a small boat, which hung down from the tip of the machine. As Jayne watched, her mouth gaping, the triangle opened up into a 3D tunnel that extended off into the distance, straight through Yolanda's bedroom wall.

Whatever that thing was, it was going to do a whole lot more than win an Invention Convention. Jayne had an awful feeling that it was about to change the world as she knew it.

When Jayne eventually took her eyes off the triangular tunnel, Yolanda was staring right at her, tongue jutting out and eyes bulging. Even though it was Yolanda's body, right there in front of Jayne, her friend was barely recognisable.

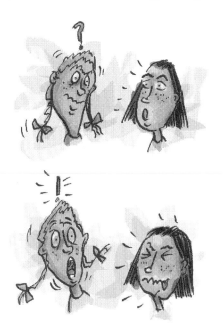

"Who you?" she said. At least that's what Jayne thought she said. She was quite hard to understand with her tongue still poking out of her mouth.

"I'm Jayne," she said, standing up and taking several steps backwards until she bumped into the computer desk. She quickly glanced out of the window in the hope that there might be someone  who could help her. The street was still empty, except for the gardener, who was now talking on her mobile phone.

"Jayne? Yeth – Yolly7 tellth me oth you. Why you are here?"

Yolly7? Oh yeah ... that was the username that Yolanda always went by.

Jayne had to do something, but she had no idea what. All she knew was that someone –

or something – had just hijacked her friend's body and opened up some sort of portal. And from what she could tell, no one else knew anything about it. At least no one on Earth, anyway. If *she* didn't stop this intruder she might never see her friend again.

"The leaders sent me," Jayne said, trying to buy herself some time to come up with a plan. "So that they could track your progress through this transmission device." Jayne nodded towards the computer.

"Leaderth?" Yolanda said. Her voice was high-pitched, her face scrunched up, and her tongue still protruding from her mouth. She didn't look at all happy. "Yolly7 broke promith. Thi thed tell no one."

"No one?" Jayne said, trying to sound as surprised as she could. "But the whole planet knows. We've all been waiting for you to succeed."

Yolanda bent forwards, her head shaking frantically like a dog trying to dry itself. Her arms swung by her side like pendulums and a long trail of saliva dripped onto the carpet. Yolanda would have died if she could see herself now.

"You planet know we ith coming?" she said to the floor, punctuating the question with another dollop of dribble.

Jayne nodded. "Yeth!"

There was a ping from the computer but Yolanda – or whatever it was in her body – did not seem to notice or care.

Jayne glanced over at the screen.

Jayne? I was tricked. Now on alien planet. They're going to invade Earth. You have to destroy machine!

So her suspicions were correct. An alien *had* swapped bodies with Yolanda. And that thing *was* a portal. But the last thing Jayne wanted to do was destroy the machine before she got her friend back. She had to trick this intruder into swapping back into its own body.

"Can the other Earthlings come in now?" Jayne asked, pointing towards the door. She had no idea what else to do, so she planned on bluffing for as long as she could. "They want to know when we can begin the evacuation!"

"Evacu-ation … the removal of persons or things from an endangered area," Yolanda said, as if reading from a dictionary.

"Yes, this planet is very endangered. It has only hours left," Jayne said, waving her hands around for added effect. "If we don't escape soon we're all going to die!"

Jayne glanced up at the new message on the computer screen. *Are you there? I've been so stupid. Please help me!*

I am trying, Yolanda, Jayne thought. *I'm doing everything I can.*

The Yolanda-invader was now shaking from head to toe. Her legs were wobbling so much that it looked like she might fall over at any moment. As far as Jayne could tell, this was how the aliens showed their emotions. And if she had to guess, she'd say this one was rather angry.

Keeping her eyes on the intruder, Jayne stretched her left hand towards the keyboard.

pyt buxket om noqw, she typed quickly, hoping that Yolanda would understand what she meant.

Car tyres screeched in the street outside the house and the Yolanda-invader flinched.

Jayne had to suppress a smile. "Ah, that will be everyone arriving," she said. "Humans are ready for the evacuation."

The invader looked around the room frantically, as if trying to find another way out. Just at that moment the portal flickered and disappeared. The machine tilted until it was vertical again.

Yolanda's body turned to look at it and suddenly stopped shaking.

Jayne couldn't believe her plan was working. If you could even call it a plan. She'd had no idea what she was going to say until the words came pouring out of her mouth.

"I mutht dethroy mathine!" the invader said, quickly looking around the room for some sort of weapon.

What? Wait ... no!

She picked the bucket off the floor and lifted it above her head, ready to smash it against the machine that was now spinning away at full speed.

"No!" Jayne said quickly, positioning herself between the bucket and the machine. "Don't destroy it. Earthlings need it to escape."

If either the bucket or the machine got damaged she might never see her friend again. Fortunately, a thought hit her before the bucket did. It was time for one final bluff.

"Actually, it's fine if you destroy that one," Jayne said. "Go ahead." She stepped aside, giving the invader full access to the whirring machine. "It's the one at the other end that we really need to protect!"

Yolanda's face scrunched up and she shook her head vigorously.

"Mutht warn all Thergkians!" she said, and she looked up at the bucket, which was glowing in her hands. She lowered it over her head without even sitting down.

Jayne backed away as the room flashed green and the piercing metallic sound filled her ears.

There was a loud thumping at the front door, as though someone was trying to break it down. Jayne didn't have time to wonder who it could be. She squatted behind the bed and watched as Yolanda's body tensed again. Her shoulders slumped and she reached up and pulled the bucket off her head, before dropping it on the floor. She looked around the room and saw Jayne peering at her over the edge of the bed.

"Jayne! You did it!" she said and she rushed towards her friend. The girls stood beside the bed hugging until the bedroom door burst open.

The first things Jayne saw were two handguns pointing right at them. One was being held by a woman wearing gardening clothes, the other by a police officer. Yolanda's dad was standing behind them, his face pale and his hands waving in the air.

"Hands above your head!" the police officer shouted, but Jayne was already stretching hers towards the ceiling. Yolanda did the same, tears streaming down her cheeks.

"What did Peter Piper pick?" the policeman barked, gesturing towards Yolanda with his gun.

Yolanda's lips parted but she didn't say anything.

The policeman asked again, more slowly this time. "What did Peter Piper pick?"

"A peck of pickled peppers?" Yolanda said, her voice high-pitched and shaky.

Jayne's breath caught in her throat as the officer trained his gun on her.

"What does she sell on the sea shore?" he asked Jayne.

"Seashells," Jayne answered automatically.

"It's okay," the lady in the gardening clothes said, lowering her gun. "They're both still human."

The policeman waited a few more seconds before lowering his weapon. Then the pair of them stepped fully into the room. When the lady saw Yolanda's machine, which was still thumping and whirring rhythmically, she let out a whistle.

"You actually got it working?" she asked. "You saw the portal?"

Both Jayne and Yolanda nodded at the same time.

"Wow, that's incredible!" the lady said, shaking her head. "This is the fourteenth invasion attempt that's been discovered, but you're the first person who's managed to make the thing work."

Yolanda looked down at her feet, her face a mixture of shame and pride. Her dad was doing his best to supress a grin.

"We're going to have to confiscate your Light Transporter," she said, waving her hand towards the machine. "And you'll both need to come into the station for questioning. But don't worry. You're not in trouble. You really have done an incredible thing. With your help we might be able to stop this threat once and for all."

Yolanda looked up at her dad for the first time, her chin trembling. Her dad walked forwards, his arms open and gave her a huge hug. "I'm sorry I've been so stupid," Yolanda sobbed, resting her face on his shoulder. Jayne stood beside them, shifting from foot to foot. She was just glad that her friend was back.

"Maybe when all this is over we can work on another invention together?" Yolanda's dad said quietly in Yolanda's ear.

Jayne smiled. She had no doubt that Yolanda would be this year's Invention Convention winner.

It's the look on Dad's face that worries me most of all. His eyes are as hard as bullets and his usual lop-sided smile has been replaced by a clenched jaw. He's breathing deeply through his nose. So deeply I can hear the wheezing from the other side of the room.

Mum had just got off the phone with Great-Aunty Sue.

"She wants to see Robert right away," she says, tilting her head to one side as if trying to get water out of her ear.

I stifle a groan. Aunty Sue is a right old bat. She's my dad's aunt and has a ton of money, yet I'm lucky if she gives me ten dollars at Christmas or on my birthday. She lives on the posh side of town in this huge house that's got more antiques in it than a museum. But I'm not allowed to touch anything. In fact, she doesn't let me out of her sight when I'm in her house, as if she's worried I'm going to break something. Plus she always fusses over me, asking if I've been eating well, getting some exercise, that kind of thing.

Dad has his hands wrapped around a coffee cup. He is squeezing it so tight I half-expect it to crack. He still doesn't say anything.

"Is this because I'm her Sole Benny-thingy?" I say.

"Sole beneficiary," Mum says. "Yes, dear, it probably has something to do with that."

I'm Aunty Sue's sole beneficiary. That means that when she dies I get all of her money and possessions. Everything.

When Dad told me a couple of years ago I nearly jumped in the air and started whooping.

Except for the look on Dad's face. He looked a bit like he does now. Like he'd just heard some really bad news.

But how bad can it be? I'm going to be extremely rich. I know they're probably just upset that she isn't giving them any money, but that doesn't matter. I plan on sharing everything with them.

"We're not going," Dad says. It's a wonder the words managed to get past his clenched teeth. They must have squeezed through the gaps.

Mum bites her bottom lip as she holds his gaze.

My heart speeds up. I can feel an argument hanging heavily in the air, like a thunderstorm. My parents don't argue much, but when they do it can get pretty loud. And it usually has something to do with Aunty Sue.

"Go and get your shoes on," Mum says to me firmly and I rush for the shelter of the hallway.

She pushes the door shut behind me. I grab my shoes and lean up against the wall, fumbling with my shoelaces. It's not easy to make a bow when your stomach is tying itself in knots.

Muffled voices slip though the crack in the door.

"I'm NOT just being paranoid!" That was Dad.

"How else are we supposed to pay his school fees?" That was Mum's voice.

It's all pretty standard stuff, so I pace up and down the hallway, trying to use heavy footsteps to drown out the rest of their words.

Eventually the door opens and they both emerge, stone-faced and silent. But they open the front door and head outside, so I guess Mum won.

As we get to the car Dad passes the keys to Mum and gets in the passenger side. It makes the volume of my heart rise a few notches. The last time Mum drove us all was when Dad twisted his ankle playing tennis. That was about four years ago.

Dad's completely silent for the first few minutes of the drive, then he goes all weird on me.

"I can't believe you had four bowls of cornflakes this morning, Robbie!"

I look at him with my eyebrows raised.

"No, I didn't, Dad. I had three bowls. Of Rice Bubbles." I swear he is losing the plot. "And you know I hate being called Robbie."

"Yeah, right. Sorry," he says, then he goes back to staring out of the window.

I feel my breath catching in my throat. Why is Dad behaving like this? We're only going to see Aunty Sue, yet he's acting like he's in a state of shock.

"I can't believe she wants to see him so late on a Sunday," Mum says. "It's so inconsiderate. She knows he has school tomorrow!"

"Mmm," says Dad, but it's like he isn't listening.

The car pulls up at a red light and Dad gets his phone out of his pocket. He looks over his shoulder at me and gives his phone a little shake. We sometimes play this game where Dad enters a phone number into his phone and I have to try to see what he's typing. It's quite good fun, now that I'm getting better at it, but I can't believe he wants to play it now.

He holds the phone in his left hand and taps in some numbers, but his right hand is completely obscuring the keys. I can't see anything.

"That's not fair, Dad," I say. "I couldn't see the keys!"

"YOU'RE RIGHT ... IT'S NOT FAIR!" Dad yells. "LIFE IS NOT FAIR!"

I hold my breath and my heartbeat fills my ears. Mum's gripping the steering wheel 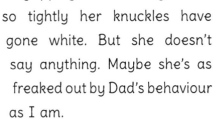 so tightly her knuckles have gone white. But she doesn't say anything. Maybe she's as freaked out by Dad's behaviour as I am.

"Sorry, Rob," Dad says quietly, taking a deep breath to calm himself down. "But I know you can do this. Have another go."

He types the number again. His hand is still blocking the keypad but I can see the slight movements of his finger and am pretty sure I know what the number is.

"3484555," I say and Dad nods in approval.

"Here's another one," he says as we pull up at another red light.

This time he rests the phone on his leg and covers it up with both hands. I can't see it at all. His hand moves as he taps at the numbers ten times. His movements are so slight it's difficult to know for sure, but I have a go anyway. I don't want him to shout again.

"022-350-2519," I say.

"NO!" he shouts. He takes another deep breath. "Try again, Rob. You can do this."

He taps out the numbers again, still keeping the phone covered so I can't see it at all. But I follow the pattern that his finger makes, and pause for a few seconds as I visualise

the keypad and work out which numbers that pattern would have pressed.

"022-350-25 … 29!" I croak, my throat dry and constricted.

Dad closes his eyes and lets out a deep sigh. But he's nodding his head ever so slightly, so I know I got it right this time.

I take a big lungful of air and let it out slowly, trying to hold the panic down. I've never seen Dad act like this before. He sits up in his seat and glances over at me, as if he's about to type another number.

"That's enough, John," Mum says, her words final.

He puts the phone back in his pocket and I feel my stomach muscles relax. I just want to get there now and prove to Dad that there was nothing to worry about. We're close already. I can tell because the houses are getting larger.

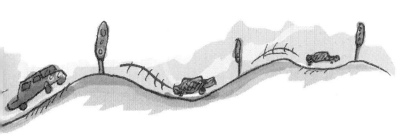

Soon we will pull into Aunty Sue's road where the houses are enormous. Hers is right at the end of the street, the biggest of all.

"Five red lights," Dad says. "I can't believe we hit five red lights today."

Neither Mum nor I respond. We pull into Aunty Sue's street and slow down over the speed bumps. Dad closes his eyes as if he doesn't want to see the house. I want to see it, though. It's going to be mine one day. Just the thought of that makes me feel a bit better, like it's worth coming out here and keeping Aunty Sue sweet, despite what Dad thinks.

Then a thought hits me. What if Aunty Sue has changed her mind? What if she's chosen a new sole beneficiary? Could that be what Dad is so upset about?

I bite my bottom lip and try not to think about it as the huge walls come into view, separated by an electric gate that looks like

it belongs at Buckingham Palace. I can just see the roof over the top of the wall, with its four chimneys pointing up at the sky. Why any house needs four chimneys I'll never know. No, in fact, hopefully I will know one day. Once the house is mine.

We are buzzed in at the gate and we pull up in front of the eight-car garage. Aunty Sue only has two cars, so I've no idea why she needs an eight-car garage. Not that I'm complaining. I plan on filling it with Porsches and Ferraris one day.

Mum is the first to get out of the car, but Dad holds back, as if he's waiting for something. Just as I pull on the door handle Dad turns around and looks at me.

He holds my gaze and I stop opening the door, my breath catching in my throat.

"Listen, Son," he says in a firm whisper. "I don't know what Aunty Sue wants today, but if she does anything strange, just call out. I'll be there in a second." He glances up as if checking that Mum is out of earshot. "And don't feel that you have to wait until the end of the meeting. It might be best if I come in a bit early!"

He carries on staring at me. I say nothing. Mostly because I've no idea what he's talking about. And because my throat is so tight I'm not sure any words would be able to escape if they wanted to. My fingers rest on the door handle for a few seconds, the thumping of my heart filling my ears.

"Let's go, Robbie," he says.

"Dad!" It's like he's doing it just to annoy me.

"Sorry, Rob," he says. "I'm sorry. I really am." Now he looks like he's about to cry.

What could possibly be making Dad freak out like this? He's never behaved this strangely before. Ever.

The front door opens and Aunty Sue is standing there, a half-smile on her face. She only ever gives you a half-smile. One side of her mouth goes up a little more than the other, and it doesn't exactly make her look happy. She looks more impatient than anything else.

"Thanks for coming at such short notice," she says, but there's no gratitude in her voice. It's like she only says it because that's what you're supposed to say.

"It's no bother at all," says Mum, giving the correct response, even though she doesn't mean it.

Dad and I don't say anything. Dad probably couldn't if he wanted to. His jaws are clamped so tight that not even the tiniest words would be able to squeeze through the gaps.

Aunty Sue is dressed in a formal outfit, like she's going to a business meeting or a funeral. Yet there doesn't seem to be anyone here, other than us. Did she get dressed up just for Mum, Dad and me?

"I've had some bad news," she says, dropping down to a quarter-smile. "I'm dying. The doctors have said there is nothing they can do. They've given me days, weeks at most."

"Oh, that's terrible!" says Mum, covering her mouth with both hands.

My jaw drops open. I can't believe it. She is going to die. In days.

I wait for tears to fill my eyes, but they don't come.

I clench my stomach, trying to force tears out. I want to cry. She is my great-aunt and has just told us that she's going to be dead in a matter of days. But the tears just aren't there.

Instead, I feel relief. Whatever Dad was worrying about, this can't have been it. And

Tom E. Moffatt

surely that means I am still her sole beneficiary. Everything is still going to come to me.

A little bubble of excitement forms in my stomach. I try to suppress it. But I feel it growing. And I hate it. I hate myself for it. But I'm thinking about the house. How the three of us could live here, instead of in our tiny place. I try to stop the thoughts, to think about how sad it is that Aunty Sue is going to die. The thing is, we almost never see her. Maybe once a year she invites us over, and it always seems like she's only doing it to check on me. She never actually talks to me or plays with me. In fact, we barely know each other at all.

Even now she's looking me up and down. It's like she's sizing me up, as you might do to a lamb you were going to slaughter.

Mum gives Aunty Sue a hug and for a second I think she's not going to let her go. It goes on for ages.

When they finish I think Dad is going to hug her too. But he just stands there, arms folded.

"So, what did you want to see us about?" he says. I feel my face flush. Surely Dad should be hugging his own aunt. It's bad that I'm not crying, but he doesn't look the slightest bit upset.

Then I remember something Mum once said. About how Aunty Sue had changed. She'd been Dad's favourite aunt when he was little, then when Dad was eleven or twelve years old, she'd witnessed her granddad's death and it completely changed her. Things between Dad and Sue had never been the same after that. I'd tried talking to Dad about it, but he would always change the subject.

Aunty Sue goes back to a half-smile. "It was Robert I wanted to see," she says, holding Dad's gaze for several seconds. "I need to discuss my estate."

I hold my breath.

Dad rubs the back of his neck. "Fine," he says in a low growl. "Discuss away."

"In private," Aunty Sue says, gesturing towards the door of her study.

Dad doesn't say anything. Mum reaches over and holds Dad's hand and I see him take a deep breath and let it out slowly.

"You can have five minutes alone," he says, staring Aunty Sue directly in the eye. "Then I'm coming in too."

Aunty Sue returns his gaze without blinking. "It will take ten minutes to work through all the documents."

Dad breathes deeply a couple more times. "Okay," he says eventually. "But you keep the door unlocked at all times."

Aunty Sue nods and gives him a half-smile.

My heart is pounding in my ears as Aunty Sue leads the way to her study. I glance over at Dad. His jaw is clenched and he is staring at us with narrowed eyes, like he doesn't want to let us out of his sight. Mum is still holding his hand and whispering something to him, probably trying to calm him down.

The thick wooden door closes with a thud and Aunty Sue reaches for the lock. She sees me staring and lowers her hand without locking the door.

But even with the door unlocked a wave of panic hits me. Why is Dad still behaving like that? Surely the fact that Aunty Sue was dying should have changed things? What does he think is going to happen?

I glance around the room, looking for signs of danger, but the study looks just like the rest of the house. There are bookshelves lined with ancient books, and a load of creepy old masks cover the walls. There's no sign of any documents.

"Sit!" Aunty Sue says, pointing at a large leather armchair with curly sides and a back that's taller than I am. "We don't have much time."

I just stand there, my back to the door and my arms hanging down by my sides. My knees feel like they might give way at any moment.

"There's no need to look so worried, Robert," Aunty Sue says. "I just want to show you my most treasured heirloom."

She points towards a large trunk on the floor that looks hundreds of years old. It's covered with amazing images, like hieroglyphics, but they're mostly of planets and stars. It's the coolest trunk I've ever seen.

"Once you've found out what's inside the trunk you'll see things quite differently." Her lips curl up into an almost complete smile and she places her hand on my shoulder, guiding me towards the chair.

I climb up into it and lean back, placing my shaking arms on the high rests. My heartbeat is still pounding in my ears, but the panic has been replaced with anticipation. I really want to know what's inside the trunk.

Aunty Sue sits opposite me in an identical chair. They've been arranged facing each other in the middle of the room with the trunk in between them. She leans back in her chair and looks at me. Really looks. As though for the first time. Then her head tips forwards and she lets out a deep puffy sigh.

"I can't believe this wretched body is failing me already," she says, more to herself than to me. "How old are you exactly, Robert? Eight? Nine?"

"I'll be eleven in March!" I say. I can't believe she doesn't even know how old I am.

"Eleven years old," she says shaking her head ever so slightly. "Oh dear, oh dear."

She removes a small metal object from her jacket pocket. It looks like a brooch in the shape of a star, but it has nine points instead of the usual five. She rests it on her forearm and pushes its centre. Aunty Sue flinches, as though she's just been pricked with a needle, and the brooch lets out a strange green glow. When she leans forwards and reaches towards the trunk the star stays there, flat against her skin like some kind of glow-tick.

I'm breathing so fast now that I'm almost panting like a dog. Part of me wants to sprint out the door and never look back. Another part is desperate to know what's in the trunk. What could Aunty Sue's most valuable heirloom possibly be?

There's a shiny star-shaped pattern on the corner of the chest closest to Aunty Sue. Just like the brooch, it too has nine points, and each of them has three shiny little indents. Aunty Sue partially covers the pattern with her left hand, and with her right she taps at the indents nine times. Then she presses the middle of the shape and there's a loud hissing noise, as though pressure is being released.

I stare with my mouth open as the top half of the trunk rises into the air. White light bursts from the edges, as though a star is trapped inside. Then I see these intricate metallic strands weaving together, forming a pillar that rises up towards me. There's another one on the other side, heading towards Aunty Sue. It looks almost like an ancient sculpture, except that it's made out of a shiny material unlike anything I've ever seen. It's a cross between metal, plastic and spiderweb.

The pillar in front of me moulds into the perfect indent of my face, like the inside of a Robert-mask. On the other side of the trunk, Aunty Sue smiles her quarter-smile as she places her face into her own mould.

I suddenly realise that I don't want to know what that thing does. I don't really know Aunty Sue. And right now, I don't trust her. I trust my dad. And he clearly thinks something bad is going to happen.

Instead of placing my face into the mould I stand up on the chair and climb over the back. If I can get to the door and back to my parents I know I'll be safe. My feet thump onto the carpet, but as I rush for the door I see a flash of silver in my peripheral vision.

I turn to see the column whipping towards me like a scorpion's tail. I cover my head with my arms and try to let out a scream to warn Dad. But the column splashes onto my face like liquid metal, muffling the sound.

I am hit by an icy sensation, as though a bucket of cold water was tipped over me. The material slithers down my throat and around the back of my head, trickling down my spine. I try to scream but no sound comes out. My heart pounds against my chest as I'm lifted into the air by my head. All I can see is a kaleidoscope of colours and patterns, swirling away in front of me, almost like a tunnel. In fact, it's exactly like a tunnel. And I'm flying through it at a million miles per hour. It's like the coolest computer game or simulator ever.

And then it stops.

It just disappears. Game over.

I feel the material retreating up my spine. Crawling off my head. Then I'm back in the chair and the metallic pillar is withdrawing into the trunk, twice as quickly as it came out. The lid hisses back down and closes with a deep thud, locking the brightness away again. The room seems darker and smaller than it was before.

My mouth is still hanging open.

The leather armchair on the other side of the trunk is empty. My own body steps out from behind the chair and stares at me with a half-smile. In fact, it's more than half. Perhaps three quarters.

"You are considerably more abiding than your great-aunt was," my own body says to me. "I actually had to strap her to this very chair."

I look down at my hands. They are large, old and a bit wrinkly. The star is glowing green on my forearm and there's a dull ache below it, as though it's digging into my bone.

My thoughts are spinning around my head. That thing inside the trunk. The tunnel of light. It swapped our bodies over. Aunty Sue is now in my body.

A realisation clicks into place. That's why I'm her sole beneficiary. Everything goes to me. But it's not me, is it? It was never going to be me. She had always planned to steal my body and take all of her possessions with her. I was only ever going to be her *soul* beneficiary. And my soul is trapped in her dying body.

"You can't do this," I say weakly, almost jumping at the sound of an old lady's voice coming out of my mouth.

"I'm afraid I already have, Robert," she says, my own voice sounding strange and cold from the outside. "Just like I did with your great-aunt Sue. And her grandfather. And his  great-uncle before that. My name is Zultan and I have been in your family for seventeen generations. Eighteen, in fact, thanks to your generosity. And it is going to be nice being male again, for a change."

My head spins and I'm struggling to breathe as I comprehend what she – or he – is saying.

"In less than eight minutes you'll be out of the equation and I will leave with my mummy and daddy."

At first I don't know what she means, then I see her glance at the star on my arm. There is still a dull ache below it and my fingers are throbbing.

Poison.

She has poisoned me so that I am out of the way and she can take my life over. I feel panic surging through me, speeding up my breathing, but I have to control myself. Panicking will only make the poison work quicker.

"But it's your wretched father I'm most worried about," Aunty Sue continues. "He's always been suspicious. He was only a child when I took over his aunt and he didn't accept that witnessing a death might change someone."

She stands up and stretches my arms out one at a time, as if testing that they work properly.

"If I could have waited until you were twenty-one years old everything would have been fine. I could have moved into this house on my own and called him a few times a year. But now he will expect to see me every day. He might figure out what's happened."

She paces around the room, as if thinking this through for the first time. The fingers on my left hand feel like they're filled with glue and the ache has reached my shoulder. I have to do something. I can't let Aunty Sue – or Zultan – get away with this. That is *my* body! But what can I do? I'm stuck in this frail body with poison rushing through my veins. I glance around the room. There are millions of books and strange wooden objects, but nothing that could get me out of this mess.

"I'll have to take him out of the equation too," my own body says, as if he were talking about putting the bins out on rubbish day. "Maybe arrange a car accident or a burglary-gone-wrong." She's talking about my father. Actually planning to kill him. Right here in front of me.

I look around the room again. I have to do something. I can't let this impostor steal my body and kill my dad. But what?

My eyes land on the trunk, which is still on the floor in front of me. I'm on the opposite side of it now and can see the keypad close up. That's the only thing that could save me. If I knew the combination pattern I might be able to swap back before this body dies. The keys are arranged in a star shape and there are no numbers on them, but I close my eyes and conjure up the image of Aunty Sue tapping out the pattern. She pressed nine times and even though she covered it up with her hands I'm pretty sure I know which ones she pressed.

But there's no way Zultan will let me activate the trunk without trying to stop me. My real body might be only ten years old but it would be able to overpower this old lady, especially now that my whole left arm has frozen up. It's rigid against my stomach with my fingers curled up into a tight claw.

I need someone to help me. Then I remember my dad. As we were getting out of the car he said, "It might be best if I come in a bit early!"

He's ready to help. In fact, I'm pretty sure he suspects that something like this might happen. That's why he didn't want me in here for long.

I'm just about to call out to him when I notice that Zultan is standing right by the door. There's no way he will let Dad in until the poison has finished me off. Right now he has my face scrunched up in concentration, as if thinking up different ways to kill my dad without getting caught. But if I shouted out he would be able to lock the door in a matter of seconds.

Then I remember the other thing Dad said. "You don't have to wait until the very end."

What does that mean? The very end for me will be when I'm dead, so I definitely don't want to wait until then.

That's it.

My dad is a genius.

The left side of this body feels like it's fallen asleep. My leg is stuck out straight with my toes curled up. I do the same to my right foot, curling the toes and sticking it out from the chair. I make my right hand into a claw, just like the left. Then I let out a low groan.

I look at my own body through half-closed eyelids and try to stretch this body's left arm out, but it doesn't work. It feels like it's glued to my stomach.

I open my mouth as if I want to say something, but don't let the words come out. Instead my head slumps forwards, my eyes closed.

"Thank the stars for that," my own voice says. Then there's a shuffling sound with some muffled grunts. I'm not sure what he's doing but I stay still, breathing slowly so that he can't see my body move.

After a few more grunts and thumps I hear heavy breathing right next to me.

I hold my breath and stay as still as I possibly can. My heart is beating so loudly in my ears I worry that Zultan will be able to hear it. He grabs my left arm and moves it, but it's locked in position next to my stomach, almost like that riggy-morty thing that dead bodies get. There's a beep and a flash of pain as he pushes the button in the middle of the star. It feels like a needle is being yanked out of the bone and I have to clench my stomach muscles to stop myself from groaning in pain.

I hear the sound of a drawer opening and something being dropped inside, followed by the door hinges creaking.

"Mummy! Daddy!" my own voice calls out urgently. "Something has happened to Aunty Sue!"

My dad is here in an instant. "Daddy's here!" he says. "What happened, Robbie?" I hear the sound of the lock clicking shut in the door, but don't know whether it was Dad or Zultan who turned it.

"I ... huh ... don't ... huh ... know!" my voice says between sobs. "It must be ... huh ... her illness, huh!" He was doing a fairly good impression of someone being upset. It just wasn't how I would have reacted. At least, not if it was Aunty Sue who had died.

"Come here, Robbie," Dad says and there's a moment's silence. I'm pretty sure that they must be hugging so I lift my head up. I don't have time to lose. This body could die on me at any moment.

"Don't call me Robbie!" I say, my voice sounding old and raspy.

Dad looks up at me. He is leaning forwards with his arms wrapped around his son. He doesn't look at all surprised that his aunt is not actually dead. In fact, he looks almost relieved.

"What did you have for breakfast?" he asks me – or his undead aunty.

"Three bowls of Rice Bubbles," I say, and he nods.

He stands, lifting my body up with him. My arms and legs are flailing about, trying to kick and punch my dad.

"PUT ME DOWN!" Zultan screams, but Dad just holds him in a bear hug.

I try to stand but the whole left side of my body has seized up and I feel myself toppling over. Pain explodes in my hip and shoulder as I slam into the floor in the middle of the room. It hurts so much that my vision turns white and for a second it feels like I'm not going to make it. As if I am going to die right there on the floor.

"Are you okay, Robert?" Dad says, an edge of panic in his voice. "Can you get to the trunk?"

"She poisoned herself," I say, my cheek pressed up against the thick carpet. "I don't have long."

Vision comes back to me slowly. The trunk has been pushed up against the wall but is only a couple of metres away. I reach out my good right arm, but the stiffness is arriving in that too. I can only stretch it a short way.

It feels like miles as I use my right arm and leg to slither along the floor. Dad can't help me. He has his work cut out just trying to keep hold of my body.

"LET GO OF ME!" Zultan shouts. "YOU WILL PAY FOR THIS!"

The trunk is close now. I reach my arm out towards the star keypad and panic wells up inside me. There are so many buttons. What if I can't remember the pattern? The pain is pouring into my right leg now. It can't be long until the poison finishes me off.

Dad is standing behind me, squeezing Zultan tight, trying to stop my body from wriggling.

"You can do it, Rob!" he says through gritted teeth, and I realise that he really believes I can. He has been training me for this moment for years.

I close my eyes, trying to visualise what it looked like when Aunty Sue pressed the different buttons on the star formation. Stretching my index finger as straight as it will go, I press the keys nine times in the same pattern. My arm falls to the floor and tiredness pulls my eyelids shut again.

I wait for the tunnel vision to return. But it doesn't come.

"WAKE UP, ROB!" Dad shouts at me. "IT DIDN'T WORK." But this time there's no anger in his voice. Only desperation.

It takes so much effort to open my eyes again it's as if my lashes have superglue on them. Dad is right next to me now and my body is still thrashing around and screaming.

"YOU WON'T GET AWAY WITH THIS!" Zultan yells.

But it's as though they're in a different dimension. I focus all of my attention on the star pattern, trying to work out what I did wrong. The buttons are so close together and there are so many that there must be thousands of possibilities.

My right index finger is bowed and throbbing, but I can just about use it. I press the centre button and there is a faint reset click. Then I tap out nine digits, making one change from last time.

Again nothing happens.

I want to cry. I want to let my eyes close and fall asleep. Forever. But I look up and see that Dad is crying. There are wide streaks of tears gushing down his cheeks.

"COME … ON … ROB!" he says between sobs. "I KNOW YOU … CAN … DO THIS!"

But I can't. I really can't. I want to close my eyes to visualise the pattern Aunty Sue made, but I am afraid I wouldn't be able to open them again. So I think through every movement. There is one option that I haven't tried that might work, but now my index finger is too curled to use. My little finger on the right hand is the only one I have left. If this doesn't work, I'm done for.

I press the centre button again and carefully move my little finger around the keypad. Five.

Six. Seven. My eyelids drop shut. My finger keeps going but I could be pressing anything. Eight. Nine.

My body slumps forwards and I wait for death to take me. In some ways I feel relieved. The pain is slipping away now, replaced by the coldness of death. I feel myself moving towards the light. But I'm going fast. Way faster than I would have imagined. Through a long tunnel.

Then my eyes are wide open and I see the silver pillars retracting back into the trunk. Aunty Sue is lying on the floor next to it, her arm outstretched. Even without checking I know that she's dead.

It's hard to breathe. Dad is gripping me so tightly that I can barely move a muscle.

"Robbie? Is that you?" he asks, his breath warm on my ear.

"Don't call me Robbie!" I say weakly, my voice hoarse from all the screaming.

Dad releases his grip slightly, but doesn't let go altogether.

"How many red lights did we hit on the way here?" he asks me.

"Five," I say and Dad places me down on the floor next to the door, away from Aunty Sue's body.

Then he collapses into one of the armchairs and covers his face with both hands. There's blood on his arms and shoulders from where I must have bitten him ... or at least Zultan must have. I would never do such a thing.

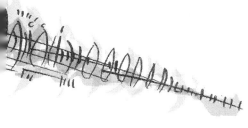

"Well done, Son," Dad says between loud sobs. He's looking at me now with tired eyes, while wiping the tear streaks away with his sleeves. "You did it."

"*We* did it, Dad!" I say, climbing up onto his lap. "You trained me well."

We sit like that for a few minutes, Dad hugging me, breathing into my hair. We are both looking down at Aunty Sue's body.

"How did you know?" I ask after several minutes of silence.

"I never knew for sure," he says, giving me a gentle squeeze. "But I had my suspicions. When Aunty Sue's granddad died she completely changed. She couldn't remember anything we'd done together and she went from visiting me every week to wanting nothing to do with me." He slips me off his lap as he stands up.

"So I started sneaking around her house, looking for clues. I knew that it had something to do with the trunk but I didn't know the code to open it." He closes his eyes and rubs his forehead, as if trying to erase a painful memory.

"I guess my aunt died a long time ago," Dad says, still staring at Aunty Sue's body as he walks towards the door. "But we need to go.

Your mum will be worried sick. And we have to start thinking about what we're going to do with your inheritance!"

The little bubble of excitement forms in my stomach again. But I don't feel guilty about it this time.

"Maybe being her sole beneficiary might not be so bad after all," I say.

As we leave the room I take a final glance over my shoulder. But I'm not looking at Aunty Sue's body. I want to see the trunk. I can't believe that that's going to be mine too.

Perhaps I should write the pattern down before I forget it.

Just in case I ever need to swap bodies.

HORSE CODE

I have to admit that the horse is pretty creepy. Its patchy brown hair clings to its body, making its bones look old and knobbly, and it won't take its beady eyes off us. But still, that doesn't explain the look on Niko's face. His mouth is gaping open and he's so pale you'd think a ghost had just flown up his nose.

"W-w-why i-is it d-d-doing that?" he stammers, while backing away slowly. I have to double-check to make sure that it's still a horse, not a fire-breathing dragon. The mangy old thing is leaning up against the fence, its eyes all bulging and unblinking, tapping its hoof on the fence rail. Tap, tap, tap ... Tap. Tap. Tap ... Tap, tap, tap.

"Doing what?" I ask. Niko can be a total wuss sometimes. The scrawny creature is just staring at us, as if we were two fat hamburgers or carrots ... or whatever it is that horses eat. Then it taps its hoof again in that same dull rhythm. Tap, tap, tap ... Tap. Tap. Tap ... Tap, tap, tap.

"That!" he says. "That tapping. That's that Morse thing that sailors do when they're in trouble. I think it's called SOS."

"Don't be ridiculous!" I say. "It's a horse, not a pirate. How the heck is it gonna know Morse code? Horse code, maybe, but not Morse code." I let out a laugh and then look down at the rock in my hand. I was about to throw it at the abandoned caravan but all the windows have been smashed anyway. The horse would make a much better target.

"Don't!" screams Niko, but he's as slow as ever. The stone is already whizzing through the air. There's a loud crack as it bounces off the fence less than a metre from the horse's head. The old nag doesn't even flinch, though. It just looks right into my eyes and makes exactly the same tapping noise. Tap, tap, tap … Tap. Tap. Tap … Tap, tap, tap. I quickly look around on the floor for an even bigger stone that will be sure to turn its tap off.

"No, Davie … don't!" says Niko again. "What if the old gypsy lady comes back?"

Trust Niko to be scared of that old hippy. "Nobody's seen her in months," I say, "and anyway … what's she gonna do? Light a few candles and flick tarot cards at me?"

I throw another stone and it curves through the air in slow motion before whacking the horse right on its neck. It doesn't hit it that hard but the skinny old thing lets out a squeal, then falls flat on its side. I'm slightly worried for a second. What if it dies and someone finds out that it was my fault? My mum would go mental. Just to be on the safe side I pull my hoodie up over my head.

"You've killed it!" says Niko. "You've only gone and killed it." The wuss actually sounds like he's about to start crying.

"It can't be dead from that little knock,"
I say. "Not even an animal as pathetic as that!"
I walk over to get a closer look. It's not moving
and I can see its ribs pushing against the skin
like a proper carcass. It can't really be dead
though, can it? I lean over the fence and try
to prod it but it's so skinny and far away that
I have to climb up onto the second rail of the
fence.

"Don't get too close!" says Niko. "What if it's
just pretending to be dead?"

He's unbelievable sometimes. "It's a *horse*,
Niko!" I say as I lean out over the fence,
stretching as far as I can. "It's even more
stupid than you are. What could it possibly do?"

At that moment the horse lunges for me. The flipping beast grabs my hood in its teeth and pulls me right over the fence. The next thing I know I'm lying on my back and its bony knees are pushing into my chest. It nuzzles its face right into mine, not biting but making this horrible slurping noise, as if it's trying to suck my face off. The smell is the worst thing ... like it's been using rotten-meat-flavoured toothpaste.

"Get off him!" Niko screams, but he sounds miles away. Out of the corner of my eye I can see him flailing his arms around and looking as scared as ever.

The horse just carries on slurping at my face. I close my eyes to make sure they aren't sucked out of their sockets and that's when the pain hits me. It's like my brain has been electrocuted. I lose my vision for a second and when it comes back I can't quite believe what I'm looking at.

It's me.

I am staring into my own face.

I stagger backwards as I watch myself, Davie Granger, get to his feet. He's wearing a weird, eerie smile that you'd never catch me wearing. It makes me look like a complete nutter.

"Are you okay, Davie?" Niko asks, but he isn't looking in my direction. He's talking to the other me … the impostor.

"I have never felt better!" the impostor says, his voice high-pitched and unnatural. Then he turns and looks straight into my eyes. "How are you feeling, little horsey? Would you like me to throw some more stones at you?"

FLEA TROUBLE

Kitur's house was perched at the top of a small hill, just like a castle. As Ben trudged up the driveway, his feet scattering gravel, he wondered what it would be like to live somewhere this posh. If he did, he would invite people up to his house every day. Show them round the rooms. Let them see all his toys and gadgets. He certainly wouldn't wait until they invited themselves. No way.

The door knocker was a golden lion with a chunky ring clenched in its jaws. As Ben grabbed hold of it and gave three loud knocks he wondered if it was made of real gold. It probably was, he decided. After all, Kitur's family could afford it.

A bearded man opened the door. Ben had never met Kitur's parents but there was no doubt that this was his dad. He had the same lanky body as Kitur and his hair stuck up from his head like bristles, just like 'Paintbrush Kit'. Obviously Kitur didn't have a beard, since he was only ten years old, but otherwise they were practically identical.

"Hi, Ben!" said Kitur's dad, a smile filling his whole face. "It's really nice that you actually came."

"Oh yeah? Erm … thanks." Ben forced a smile and wondered what exactly Kitur had told his parents. He couldn't help feeling a bit guilty about inviting himself over. "Is Kitur in?"

"It's me!" said Kitur's dad, patting his large chest with both palms. "It's Kit. My father's just borrowed my body to do some work on his car. Apparently these hands are too big to get right into the engine." As he said it he waved his hairy hands in front of Ben's face.

"Oh, right," said Ben, backing his head away from the strange man's hands. Then he bit down on his bottom lip to stop a smile from lighting up his face. He had definitely not forgotten that the family had a mind-swapping machine. Why else would he choose to spend time with Paintbrush Kit outside of class?

"Come in!" Mr Kumar – or Kitur – said, leading the way to the kitchen through a grand hallway that was nearly the size of Ben's whole house. He picked a bowl of ice cream up from the counter and shovelled a spoonful into his mouth. "You want some?" he asked, the ice cream sloshing around visibly on his tongue. A large dollop slipped from his mouth and disappeared into his beard.

Ben shook his head. He would have loved some ice cream but he didn't want to push his luck. Especially not when everything was looking so good. He couldn't believe that Kitur was actually in his dad's body. Surely that meant that he'd have to swap back at some point, so Ben might get to see the machine in action. Imagine that! He would be the envy of the whole school. The whole country, even. "When are you swapping back into your own body?" he asked, keeping his voice as flat and steady as he could.

"I'm not sure," Kitur said. "Not until much later, I imagine. The deal is that once Father's finished on the car he's got to wash my hands properly, because it's a nightmare getting engine grease off. Then after we switch back I'm allowed more ice cream, since technically speaking I haven't had any yet."

He spooned the last dollop of ice cream into a big smile, then attempted to lick the bowl. Although all he really did was clean it on his beard. "Would you like to check out the mind-swapper?"

Ben nodded immediately, then cursed himself for being too enthusiastic. He needed to look like he was here to hang out with Kitur, but this was just too exciting. Not to mention slightly confusing, with Kitur in his dad's body.

"Oh, you know ..." Ben said as casually as he could. "Only if you want to."

"Why not!" the man said, his voice just a little too loud and high-pitched for an adult. "I'll show you how it works!" He turned and strode down a long corridor with lots of doors on either side. When he reached one halfway down he grabbed the handle and slowly pushed it open.

Ben struggled to keep up with Kitur's dad's long legs. He rushed along behind him, then held his breath as he peered into the room.

Kit enjoyed watching Ben's face as he stepped into the games room. His lips were parted and his eyebrows raised so high you'd think the room was filled with gold bullion.

He turned to look at the mind-swapping machine himself. It was indeed a marvel of modern science, yet his father had bought it home from work three weeks ago, so he was now used to having it around. Anyone could tell that it was built by the Odawara Technology Company. The bulk of the metal machine was their trademark maroon colour, edged with

the usual dazzling chrome. And their logo took centre place, like an enormous car badge.

This particular model was the smallest that OTC sold and was roughly the size and shape of an old arcade machine. The two throne-like chairs protruded from either side, and above each of them hung the proton tubes – two metal funnels that resembled ornate shower heads. When his father had first bought it home Kit had stared at it for hours, asking questions, trying to figure out how it worked. Now he almost took it for granted.

Ben, however, did not look like he was taking it for granted. He looked like he was about to bow down and start worshipping it.

"Do you want to have a go?" Kit asked in his manly voice.

Ben's eyes opened even wider and his lips moved as though he were trying to speak but someone had pushed the mute button.

Kit knew that he really shouldn't let Ben have a go. His father would kill him if he found out that he'd used it unaccompanied by an adult. But it was great having someone visit him on the weekend. Plus Ben had been talking to him at school considerably more than usual. If he let him have a go on the mind-swapper perhaps they might even become proper friends.

"Could I? Really? With your dad's body?" Ben said, unable to hide his enthusiasm. It was impossible to play it cool with the mind-swapper sitting right there, in the same room.

"You can have a go …" Kitur said the words slowly as if he was about to change his mind. Ben's breath caught in his throat. He'd kick himself if Kitur changed his mind just because he'd been too keen. "The thing is," Kitur continued, "it's against the law to swap with someone who's not in their own body. It gets too complicated getting back to normal. Why don't you swap with the cat instead?"

Kitur pointed at a large ginger cat that was slumped on an armchair in the corner of the room, nibbling at its own leg.

Ben's mouth dropped open. "Erm, yeah!" he said quickly. Then he added, "If it's not too much hassle!"

Not only was he about to try out an Od-Tech mind-swapper, he was also going to have a go in a cat's body. What a result that Mrs Tamaki had made them work together last week, otherwise he might never have known that Kitur even had a mind-swapper.

"It's no hassle at all, mate," Kitur said with a big smile. He pushed a button on the control panel and one of the chairs folded over, small motors whirring away as side panels emerged out of nowhere. Within a few seconds the chair had been replaced by a waist-height box with low sides.

Ben couldn't believe how cool this machine was. He reached out a hand and pressed his fingers against the cold metal. The vibrations made his skin tingle and he closed his eyes so he could enjoy the sensation, blocking out Paintbrush Kit and his fancy house. He just wanted to feel like he was alone with the machine, as though it belonged to him.

When Ben opened his eyes Kitur's dad – or Kitur – was placing the cat into the newly-formed box. He fastened a clip around its collar and stroked it with his large hairy hands. The cat seemed completely unfazed, as though it had done this many times before. It merely scratched itself behind the ear.

Ben stood staring at the cat, jiggling his leg with excitement. Those gleaming eyes that could see in the dark. Sharp claws for climbing trees. Oh, the fun to be had.

"Aren't you going to sit down?" Kitur asked, nodding his dad's head towards the other chair.

Ben blinked a few times, trying to shake himself out of a daydream involving a very tall tree, then he rushed over to the other side of the mind-swapper and lowered himself into the seat.

"I'm going to strap you in properly, if that's all right? Otherwise Ninja might try to dash out of the room in your body, and we wouldn't want to break the cat flap, would we?" Kitur slapped his thigh and let out the loud high-pitched laugh that everyone made fun of at school.

With another press of a button, solid metal straps came out of the arms and legs of the chair. As Ben arranged his limbs in place, each strap snapped shut and tightened automatically.

"You ready?" Kitur asked.

Ben nodded quickly, urging him to get on with it. He could no longer see the cat from where he was sitting but he could hear the sound of its collar jangling as it scratched itself. Then he heard the clicking sound of Kitur pressing the activation button.

There was a rumbling from deep inside the machine, like gears grinding together. The mind-swapper started to shake, jerkily at first, then building into a smooth vibration that Ben could feel through every bone in his body.

A strange buzzing sound came from the funnel above his head, quickly growing into a static roar. Ben could feel his hair standing up, as if being sucked into the machine. The pull seemed to grab hold of his brain, forcing his eyes to roll back in his head. There was a brief burst of pain, then nothing.

The deep rumbling slowed, until all that could be heard from the mind-swapper was a faint hum. At first everything appeared normal to Kit. The readout on the screen showed that the minds were successfully swapped. Ben's mouth had dropped open and his tongue was jabbing at thin air, but that was what happened when an animal had a go in a human body.

Then he looked at the cat. It was sitting in the containment box, casually licking its paw. On the weekend that his father had first bought the mind-swapper home everyone had had a go in the cat's body. Even his grandmother had had a turn. Kit had seen all of his family members running around as the cat, and he'd had four or five goes himself. But none of them – not one – had at any point licked themselves. It was just a little too gross, even from a cat's-eye perspective.

"Ben?" he said, looking deep into the cat's eyes. The cat let out a yawn and scratched behind its ears.

A very bad feeling started in Kit's gut and rose into his chest. If Ben's mind was not in the cat, then where had it gone? It was clearly no longer in his real body, which looked like it was trying to lick its own nose.

MIND SWAP
COMPLETE

Kit glanced at the words 'Mind-swap Complete' on the screen, before looking back at the cat. It stopped scratching and looked around the room thoughtfully, its eyes bright and intelligent.

A surge of relief washed over Kit. Perhaps Ben's mind was in Ninja's body after all.

Then the cat pointed its hind leg towards the ceiling and licked its own testicles.

Ben knew that something was wrong as soon as his vision came back. He wasn't sitting in the shallow box. In fact, he didn't know where he was. It looked like some kind of forest. There were thick trunks all around him, closer together than any trees he'd ever seen. He stared around in horror, trying to work out where he could be.

That was when he saw it. An alien creature as big as him with a row of fangs like daggers was standing just a few trees away from him. It had these strange needles poking out from below its fangs. And there were thick hairs all over its body.

Had he been transported to another planet?

Before he was able to let out a scream an enormous object smashed through the trees. It was like a giant claw covered in the same orange forest. One of the car-sized sharp bits smashed into the alien, squishing him into the ground. The claw lifted up again, then came crashing back down. Up and down it went, tearing through the trees, getting closer and closer to Ben.

He dived out of the way and found himself gliding through the trees, as though he was swimming through water.

Suddenly a deep, booming voice filled the whole world, as though God himself were speaking.

"BEN? WHERE THE HECK ARE YOU?" it bellowed.

It seemed to be coming from above, so Ben turned and started gliding up towards the sound. More and more light filtered through the trees as they thinned out around him.

Suddenly Ben arrived at the treetops, and he instantly froze in shock. Right above him, as tall as the Empire State Building, was Kitur's dad's head. His ginormous mouth opened and he spoke again, the words vibrating through Ben's entire body.

"YOU'VE GOT TO BE HERE SOMEWHERE! THE MACHINE SAYS THE SWAP WAS SUCCESSFUL."

Ben couldn't take his eyes off Kitur's dad's teeth. Each one was as big as a house.

"I'm right here!" Ben tried to say, but no sound came out. Instead five long needles protruded from his face and waved from side to side. He turned away from the massive head and looked around, frantically trying to work out what was happening.

Not far beyond the sloping ginger jungle he could see a high wall. There was a thick harness stretching from the wall to a point just below a huge cat's ear. He suddenly realised where he was. He was actually sitting on top of the cat, inside the mind-swapping box. But if he was on top of the cat, then whose mind had he swapped with?

He lifted his four arms in front of his face. His four arms! Four tiny arms and powerful back legs. Ben was a flea. He had swapped bodies with a flea!

Kit's breath sped up and his heart pounded in his ears. His parents were going to kill him.

They'd specifically told him not to go near the mind-swapper unsupervised. Not ever. Never.

"It can be very dangerous," Father had said, "if you're not one hundred per cent sure of what you are doing."

"Not to mention the fact that your father could well lose his job at OTC if some mind-swapping muddle were to be splattered all over the news," Mother had said. "It's just not worth the risk!"

Kit chewed his thumbnail as he looked down at the cat. He didn't get it. Ben's mind had to have gone somewhere. The cat scratched itself on the neck a couple of times then continued licking its testicles. Either Ben had lost his mind, or Kit had lost Ben's mind. And neither circumstance would look good for his father's job.

There was a long gargling sound from the other side of the mind-swapper. Kit spun around to look at Ben's body. His tongue was poking out and his eyes were rolling around in his head like a couple of marbles. Whenever it was in a human body the cat usually just stared around the room making weird groaning noises. Anyway, surely the cat was still in its own body. Why else would it lick its own private parts?

In that case, what on earth was in Ben's mind now?

As Kit stared with wide eyes Ben jerked his knees from side to side with such force that the whole machine shook. If he kept that up he would rip the leg supports right off the chair. A red splotch appeared on Ben's trouser leg from where the strap was digging into his skin. But even that didn't stop him. He just seemed to kick even harder. Then he started opening and closing his mouth. The problem was that his tongue was still poking out. If he wasn't careful he was going to bite it clean off.

Kit had to do something, but what? There was only one thing he could think of. He had to reverse the process before whatever-it-was did any more damage to Ben's body. He rushed over to the control panel, scrolled down to 'revert', then tapped the 'search' button.

The loading bar appeared on the screen, like it always did when it was searching for the correct minds. However, this time it took ages.

Kit's breath was heavy and his chest kept getting tighter as he waited for the machine to lock onto the right minds. Eventually there was a dinging sound and the screen said, 'Target locked.'

He let out a huge sigh of relief.

The cat was scratching itself again and Ben's knees were now banging together as his legs thrashed about. But the machine never lied. It must have locked onto the same minds. This would all be over in a moment.

Kit slapped the green button and took a step back.

The humming sound seemed to fill the whole world this time and Ben could feel the pull at his head again. The mind-swapping machine must have locked onto his mind and was about to swap him back.

Thank goodness.

He didn't want to spend another second as this disgusting flea. And he certainly didn't want the flea driving his own body for any longer. He couldn't see what it was doing but Kitur's dad seemed pretty shocked every time he looked in that direction.

The noise had become deafening and Ben could feel his eyes rolling. Any second now and the pain would hit. But this time it would be welcome.

Just as his vision began to fade Ben saw movement above him. He turned his body in time to see the cat's claw coming down at him like an aeroplane falling out of the sky.

He raised his four arms up over his face in a feeble effort to protect himself. Just as the claw was about to crush him Ben kicked with his hind legs.

Suddenly he was flying through the air as though he had been shot from a cannon. He flew over the edge of the box, right into the middle of the room. After spinning through the air a few times he landed perfectly on the floor, waving his front arms to keep his balance.

The noise of the machine died down and the room filled with silence.

An ice-cold feeling rose up from the very centre of Ben's flea body. He had missed the switch. He was now in the middle of the room, perched on top of a beige mound that looked like a haystack. Carpet. He was on a tuft of carpet.

Suddenly, the light dimmed.

Ben glanced behind to see Kitur's dad stomping across the room. He was absolutely

enormous, like fifty Statues of Liberty stacked on top of each other.

A foot the size of a car ferry was coming down towards Ben. He quickly kicked his legs and shot sideways, but the foot was too big. Its rubber sole descended upon him and the whole world went black.

∼∿∿∿

Kit rushed towards the machine as soon as it quietened down. He could feel his breathing slowing as he started to relax. *Surely this will have worked?*

Everything looked okay. Both Ben and the cat were sitting quietly, their eyes slowly taking in their surroundings. Then the cat gave an enormous kick, its legs jerking forwards. There was a thud as the harness tightened and the cat landed on its back, its back legs still swiping at the air.

At that moment Ben let out a high-pitched squeak that sounded like air being squeezed from a rubber toy. His eyes darted around the room and his arms and legs jolted, making the red patch on his trouser-leg spread.

An apple-sized lump rose into Kit's throat and the corners of his mouth quivered.

What had happened now? It didn't make any sense. Father had said that the machine was programmed to always revert people back to their own bodies. So what the heck had happened this time?

Tears streamed from his eyes, rushing down his cheeks and into his beard. His stupid beard. Kit couldn't believe that on top of all this craziness, he was still inside his father's body.

Ben let out another squeal, even louder than the last, and it was more than Kit could handle. He rushed up to the machine, his arms flailing.

"Just put them back to normal!" he screamed, then he whacked the green button with all his might.

But he'd forgotten his father's strength.

The button made an awful crunch, before falling off and rolling across the floor. Kit looked on through blurry eyes as the machine whirred to life. The rumbling sound got louder and louder as though it was about to swap minds again.

Panic clawed its way up Kit's throat. The stupid machine had messed things up enough before it had malfunctioned. What was it going to do now? He couldn't let things get any worse, so he rushed towards Ben and hit the release button on the back of the chair. The straps clicked open but Kit couldn't hear the sound over the thunderous roar emanating from the machine.

He grabbed Ben's body and easily lifted him out of the chair. As he dragged him to safety there was a thumping, grinding sound, like a washing machine full of bricks. The word

'MALFUNCTION' flashed across the screen and smoke began to pour out of both funnels.

The screen went blank and silence filled the room. Kit gently lowered Ben to the ground and then slumped down onto the carpet, letting out huge snotty gasps. Tears streamed from his eyes. What on earth had he done now?

The cat clambered away, rushing towards the cat flap as fast as Ben's body could crawl.

There was nothing Kit could do but watch as Ben's head rammed into the door. Ben yelped, before backing up and trying again. There was no yelp this time. Just a sickening crunch. Ben's body collapsed in a heap on the floor.

Kit rested his face in his hands and sobbed, taking big raspy breaths that hurt his throat. How could things have gone quite so badly? All he'd wanted to do was impress Ben with the mind-swapping machine. And now he had no idea if Ben would ever be himself again.

Through the blurry gap between his fingers Kit saw something land on his leg. At first he thought it was a fly and he waved his hand to scare it away.

But it wasn't a fly. It was way too small. It was a flea. That blasted cat must have gotten fleas again.

As quick as he could Kit swung his hand around and slapped his leg, trapping the flea beneath his fingers.

He got it. He'd actually caught it. At least he could do something right.

Kit pinched the flea between two fingers and brought it up to his face. The pathetic little creature was still wriggling around, trying to get away. He squished it with his fingernail until it stopped moving. Then he flicked it across the room.

It was the last time that silly little thing would bother him!

~~~~~~

Kitur is an idiot. An absolute plonker. What the heck was he doing, squishing me like that?

These were the first thoughts that came to Ben's mind as he slipped back into consciousness. His head was spinning and his whole body throbbed with pain. He didn't open his eyes, because he didn't have any eyelids. But after a while the darkness faded, leaving him staring up at three ginormous figures. As the haze cleared from his head the booming words that had been filling the room began to sink in.

"DO YOU KNOW HOW MUCH TROUBLE YOU ARE IN, YOUNG MAN?" Kitur's mum was saying, wagging her finger directly at Kitur's dad's chest. The patches of cheek above his beard glistened as he hung his head.

Ben remained on his back in the middle of the carpet, watching the enormous human beings towering above him.

"WHAT ARE WE GOING TO DO, RANJIT?" Kitur's mum asked, turning to face her son's body. "WE CAN'T TAKE THAT BOY BACK TO HIS PARENTS LOOKING LIKE THAT. THEY'LL HAVE A FIT!" She pointed towards Ben's body, which looked absolutely nothing like the person Ben saw every time he looked in the mirror. He was lying on his back next to the door, sniffing at the air with his face scrunched up and his teeth bared. There was a huge red bump on his forehead.

Kitur was staring at the mind-swapping machine with his hands on his head. "THIS THING'S TOTALLY RUINED," he said. "IT'LL TAKE ME MONTHS TO FIX. AND IF I DON'T GET EVERYONE BACK IN THEIR OWN BODIES TODAY MY JOB WILL BE HISTORY."

Kitur's dad let out another sob and wiped his nose on the back of his hand. Then he casually flicked his wrist, sending a huge droplet of snot flying through the air. The enormous snot-comet splatted down onto the carpet, close to where Ben was lying.

Ben tried to push himself up with his four arms. He'd already been stepped on and squished, and now he was in danger of getting snotted. He had to get to a safer part of the room but one of his hind legs was hanging limply behind him and he fell flat on his back.

"BUT HOW ARE WE GOING TO GET EVERYONE BACK TO NORMAL WITHOUT THE MIND-SWAPPER?" Kitur's mum asked.

Kitur squeezed his lips together as he stared into space. 'WE'RE GOING TO HAVE TO GO

INTO WORK," he said, rubbing his temples with his thumbs. "THERE'S A SIX-WAY MIND-SWAPPER IN MY BOSS'S OFFICE. WE'LL JUST HAVE TO HOPE THAT HE'S NOT THERE TODAY."

"WELL, LET'S GET EVERYTHING WE NEED AND GET THIS OVER WITH AS SOON AS POSSIBLE," Kitur's mum said, before turning towards the door.

Ben froze. From where he lay Kitur's mum was as tall as Mount Everest. And she was wearing shoes that gave a new meaning to the words 'high heels'. The pointy bits alone were each the size of a skyscraper. They thumped past Ben, leaving a line of craters behind them. Ben pushed himself up again, this time managing to stay upright, but his hind leg was too damaged to jump. He hobbled along as fast as he could, trying to get out of the way before Kitur's mum returned with those killer shoes.

The mounds that made up the carpet were three times higher than Ben's flea-body. With one of his hind legs hanging limply he was forced to crawl up each mound and slide down the other side. Once he'd cleared ten of the hills he stopped at the top to see how far he'd come. His heart sank. The pool of snot was still glistening close by. He could only have travelled a couple of centimetres. The room spread out into the distance, with the mind-swapping machine towering above the horizon like a man-made mountain.

Kitur opened up a compartment on the mind-swapper that Ben hadn't even known was there. He removed a small metallic cylinder, placed it inside a case and slipped it into his pocket. He then strode across the room. He was far enough away that Ben didn't need to panic but he could feel the floor shake as huge feet thumped against the carpet.

When he arrived at the back door Kitur's dad bent down and tried to lift Ben's body from the floor. However, he must have forgotten that he was in a ten-year-old's body. Ben watched his own body slip from Kitur's grasp and bump down onto the floor.

"HELP ME OUT, WOULD YOU?" Kitur's dad called to his son who was slumped up against the far wall. He had puffy red eyes and bits of snot clumped in his beard.

Kitur strode over and was able to lift Ben's body and fling it over his shoulder with ease. The cat screeched and clawed at Kitur's dad's bottom, but human fingernails weren't as sharp as the claws it was used to.

A loud clomping sound made Ben spin around just in time to see Kitur's mother hurrying across the room. She was heading straight towards the tuft of carpet that Ben was perched on. In her hand she held a cat carrier the size of an aircraft hangar, but Ben was paying way more attention to the towering red shoes that were heading right for him.

He took a step backwards and slipped, tobogganing down the mound on his hard shell. He landed in a heap at the bottom, looking straight up at the towering stiletto heel that was bearing down on him. It was going to crush him at any moment.

Ben's one good hind leg was spring-loaded underneath him. Just before the huge cylinder squashed him into the floor Ben released his leg. It flung him out of the way, spinning him around like a Frisbee. The giant legs and carpet whizzed past his eyes until he landed with a splash, right in the middle of the pool of snot.

The stilettos continued their journey across the carpet, leaving Ben alive, but covered in sticky mucus. He tried kicking his good leg again but the snot was so thick that he didn't even move. All he could do was lie there and look up at the giants as they got ready to leave the house without him.

Kitur was still carrying Ben over his dad's shoulder, while his dad – still in Kitur's body – unstrapped the cat-flea from its harness. It was all very confusing and Ben doubted that even a six-way mind-swapper would be able to undo this mess. Especially not if he was still lying here in the snot puddle.

Kitur's mum put the cat carrier down on the carpet and opened the hatch on the top.

There was a sudden ear-piercing screech. The cat, who was in Ben's body, had just seen the carrier and let out a half-human, half-feline yowl. It swung its arms around and kicked its legs in a total frenzy, clearly thinking it was being taken to see the vet. Kitur was clutching it over his shoulder but the movement was just too much. From his snot-pool on the carpet Ben could see Giant Kitur swaying and he knew exactly what was going to happen.

Kitur took several steps into the middle of the room before his legs buckled. He fell onto his knees, then almost in slow motion, his whole body tipped forward. All Ben could see was Kitur's dad's giant head and his own giant bottom come crashing down on him.

Mother kept glancing over her shoulder and peering into the cat carrier that was between Ben's body and Kit on the back seat. The cat was lying on its side with its tongue poking out and its hind legs jerking back once in a while. She'd then turn her wrinkled brow back to the road and chew her lip for a few moments. Eventually she said, "Your friend doesn't like being a cat very much."

Kit didn't say anything but his heart thumped so loudly in his chest that he would've had to shout to be heard over the top of it. He knew that he should tell his parents that it wasn't actually Ben's mind in there. But he had no idea where it had gone and he certainly didn't want to admit that he had lost it. He was in enough trouble already. Of course, they were going to find out eventually, weren't they? Kit tried not to think about that.

He shuffled around on the back seat attempting to get his long legs comfortable.

He should really be sitting in the front since he was in a grown-up's body, but his father wouldn't hear of it. In fact, Father had insisted that he drive the car at first, but Mother had talked him out of it because while he was still in Kit's body he didn't technically have a driver's licence. So now Kit was stuck in the back with no leg room, the cat carrier wedged in next to him and Ben-cat writhing around and making high-pitched whining noises. Ben was strapped into his seatbelt, so hopefully Ninja wouldn't do any more damage to his body. Yet he was clawing at the window and pressing his face up to the glass, so Kit really hoped they didn't drive past anyone who recognised him.

They travelled in silence for a few minutes. At least, no one spoke. There was still the sound of the cat thrashing around inside the carrier and a low whimpering from Ben-cat as he licked the window.

"We're nearly there,' his father said, as they drove into the Odawara Technology entrance. "Can you remember what you need to say?"

Kit nodded. He'd been running through his lines in his head for the last few minutes.

They pulled up at the guard station and Kit wound his window down. It was stupid that he was in the back. This would have been much more convincing if he'd been sat in the passenger seat. Or even the driver's seat, although perhaps that wouldn't have been such a good idea.

"You're slouching, Kit. Sit up straight!" Mother whispered as the guard walked over to the car.

Kit puffed his chest out and tried to act like his father.

"Hello," he said, keeping his face nice and stern. "I'm here to pick up my UBS drive."

The guard looked at him blankly.

"USB," said the boy in the front seat.

"USB," Kit repeated. "I am here to pick up my *USB* drive."

The guard lowered his head and stared into the vehicle. Kit kept his back straight and his head elevated. He glanced to the side to see what Ben was up to, then wished that he hadn't. Ben was leaning forwards and licking his own leg. There was a long piece of dribble dangling from his mouth.

The guard stood up straight, a forced smile on his face. "Very well, Mr Kumar," he said. "And good day to the family."

"Good day to your family too," Kit said, trying to sound like a grown-up.

Mother pulled away a little too quickly and the last thing Kit saw was the guard narrowing his eyes as the car drove off.

"Right," said Father as they pulled up outside the

main doors. "Kitur, you'll have to carry your friend's body. Tanvi, you grab the cat carrier. I'll lead the way. And if anyone stops us, don't forget we're here to pick up my *USB* stick."

Fortunately it was Saturday, so there weren't too many people milling around when they got out of the car. Kit grabbed Ben's body in an outward-facing bear hug and then followed his own body through the sliding doors. He'd never actually seen himself from behind before and he didn't realise he had curly tufts of hair along his neckline. He watched his own body reach up and press the lift button.

The lift doors jolted open and the family shuffled in. Kit flinched at the reflection he saw in the mirrored walls. Instead of his usual ten-year-old self he could see his father's bearded face, and his hairy arms gripping his friend's writhing body. Ben-cat didn't seem to like what he saw either. He let out a yowl and swung his head about as though trying to wriggle free. Kit tightened his grip and spun around so that neither of them had to look at their reflections.

Just as the doors started to close a tall Japanese lady in an immaculate blue dress rushed over and stopped the door with her foot.

Kit's mother pressed the 'open' button and smiled at the lady as she joined them in the lift.

"Hello, Kumaru-San," the lady said to Kit through a big, toothy smile. "Is this your wife?"

Kit glanced over at his mother, who was nodding profusely.

He nodded too, and tightened his grip on Ben-cat.

"This is Mu... Tanvi," he said. The two ladies shook hands and smiled at each other. There was silence as the doors closed. It felt like everyone was waiting for Kit to say something but he had no idea what.

"I am Mr Tanaka's wife, Sachiko?" the lady said eventually.

Kit's father was shuffling uncomfortably from one of Kit's feet to the other. His face had gone bright red. He pressed the button for Floor 27 and then looked down at his shoes.

"That's where I'm going too," the lady said.

Suddenly Kit realised why his father looked so uncomfortable. This was his boss's wife. And she was going up to the same office as them. How could they possibly swap back into their own bodies if she was there too?

No one spoke as the lift began its ascent. Fortunately, Ben-cat stopped writhing around and started to relax. Then there was a sound like air being released from a balloon.

"Thfffffft!"

The cat had become too relaxed.

Mrs Tanaka coughed into her hand as an awful smell filled the lift. Kit grimaced and felt his eyes fill up with water.

The numbers on the lift lit up to show their progress; 9, 10, 11.

But it wasn't fast enough. The smell was so bad that Kit could barely breathe. Mrs Tanaka shot her arm out and hit the button for Floor 12.

The lift doors opened, letting in a gust of fresh air. "I forgot to get something from the … ummm … storeroom!" she said, rushing off down the corridor without looking back.

The doors closed, but the smell was not so bad as they continued up to the twenty-seventh floor. Kit was relieved that Mrs Tanaka had got out of the lift, but he still flinched every time there was a thud from the cat carrier. His mind was racing. Should he warn his parents that something had gone wrong with Ben's swap? Or should he just wait until afterwards, when they would be able to see for themselves?

The elevator doors swung open, as if answering the question for him. Kit's father rushed over to the large double doors at the end of the corridor. There was a golden plaque outside that said, 'Executive Director's Office'.

His father typed a PIN code into a keypad and pushed the doors open. When he stepped into the office Kit let out a gasp. The mind-swapper they had at home was pretty awesome, but this one was something else. It filled the whole length of the office and was one of the most dazzling things Kit had ever seen. It was almost entirely constructed out of a metal so shiny that you could have brushed your hair in front of it.

Father rushed over to the machine and pulled the mind-swapping disk out of his pocket. He placed it into a reader slot and pressed a few buttons to bring the machine to life. Kit could hear him still tapping away at the buttons as he dropped Ben's body down into one of the seats and activated the restraints. The cat thrashed around and hissed in his face, but with his mother's help Kit was able to get Ben-cat secure.

It was a bit easier with the cat's body, since they were able to plop the carrier down directly on the seat.

"That doesn't make sense," Kit's father said. "The machine says that it needs to make four swaps, rather than just two."

Kit shifted on his father's large feet. He should have come clean earlier. Of course the disk would tell Father exactly what had happened. He let out a deep breath. It was time to tell them the truth.

Before he had a chance to say anything, Kit-Father spoke. "A flea?" he said, his eyes still scanning the screen. "The boy swapped bodies with a flea?"

Kit gasped a big, raspy breath.

Oh no!

What if …

No, no, no.

It couldn't be.

Ben couldn't have been the flea that Kit killed, could he?

Tears welled up in his eyes again.

He had killed Ben.

With his bare hands!

"Did you know about this?" Kit-Father asked, looking straight into Kit's eyes.

Kit felt a tear trickle down his cheek and into his beard. He opened his mouth to confess, but there was a click on the other side of the room. He turned his head to see Mrs Tanaka, framed in the doorway. Standing in front of her was a Japanese man with a grey suit and matching grey streaks in his hair. He was staring straight at Kit and there was so much power in his eyes that Kit felt himself wilting.

"Kumaru-San!" the man barked. "What you all doing in my office?"

Kit's mouth dropped open even further. What was he supposed to say? Surely the USB excuse would not work now. And from the look on his own face Kit could tell that his father was panicking too. His eyes were blinking frantically and his mouth was flapping open and closed.

Before Kit had a chance to respond his father reached his arm out and slapped the revert button.

Whose was that other voice? And why had everyone gone silent?

From Ben's position in Kitur's dad's hair he could hear everything that was going on, but he couldn't see a thing. And he didn't want to risk moving to the outside of the hair. No way. He was safe where he was. And he was very thankful that Kitur had fallen on top of him. Otherwise he'd still be lying in that pool of snot.

A deep humming sound rose up around him, filling the entire universe with vibrations. Was that the mind-swapper? Had they pressed the button already?

As if to answer the question Ben felt his head being drawn upwards, as though a ginormous vacuum cleaner was sucking him up. He held himself completely still, not wanting to do anything that might jeopardise the switch.

There was a sharp jab of pain in the very centre of Ben's head. White light flashed across his vision, then Ben found himself sitting in a large metal chair. He tried to lift his hand to his face to examine it but his arm was strapped to the chair. His legs were tied down too and they throbbed with pain underneath the harnesses.

But everything else felt and looked normal. Could he really be back in his own body?

Ben glanced around the room. There was a Japanese couple standing by the doorway, staring at Kitur's dad. The man's lips were squeezed together and his nostrils were flaring. Ben felt his stomach clench in worry.

"Kumaru-San, is that you in there?"

"Yes, Tanaka-San," Kitur's dad said. "You have my humblest apologies." He bowed down low, a very serious expression covering his face.

"I am sure you aware of the consequences of misusing our equipment, Kumaru-San."

Kitur's dad nodded. "Yes, sir. My son used the machine unaccompanied, but I accept full responsibility for his actions."

"If I receive your resignation in writing tomorrow morning I not feel it necessary to press charges."

Resignation? Resigning? Surely he didn't mean that Kitur's dad had to quit his job? Ben felt a tingling sensation in his chest and breathing became difficult.

"Yes, sir," said Kitur's dad again. "I will hand my notice in first thing in the morning.'

Kitur let out a loud sniff. Ben could not see him from where he was sitting but he was certain that he was crying.

But this wasn't Kitur's fault, was it? It was Ben's fault. And now Kitur's whole family was being punished.

"Excuse me, sir," Ben said, his voice squeaking like a rusty gate. "But this wasn't Kitur's fault. Or his dad's."

Silence filled the room and everyone's eyes were on Ben. He gulped and took a deep breath. He couldn't turn back now.

"It was all my fault, sir. When I heard that Kitur had a mind-swapping machine at home I started being nice to him. I invited myself to his house." There were tears streaming down Ben's cheeks now. "Kitur only used the machine to impress me. If anyone should be punished it should be me, not Kitur or Mr Kumar." Ben sniffed hard to stop the snot from dripping from his nose. "I'm so sorry," he added. He could feel Kitur's whole family staring at him, but he kept his eyes firmly on the floor just below Tanaka-San's feet. He didn't want to have to meet anyone's gaze.

There was a moment of silence but to Ben it felt like hundreds of years. He glanced up at the man's face. His eyes were narrowed and his eyebrows lowered in concentration. Then he nodded his head once and turned to face Kitur's dad.

"Very well, Kumaru-San. I take boy's word this time. You keep your position."

Ben closed his eyes and let out a huge sigh of relief.

"However, your mind-swapping machine will be collected this afternoon and you not permitted to keep one on your premises in the future."

A few moments later Kitur's family, Ben and the cat were standing in the lift once again, this time in their own bodies.

"I'm sorry your mind-swapping machine is getting taken away," Ben said, his voice only just audible above the humming of the descending lift. He didn't take his eyes off of his own reflection, as though afraid it might change if he looked away.

"I don't think that's going to be a problem at all, Ben," Kitur's dad said. "We've had enough body swaps to last us a life time."

"Thank you for telling the truth up there," Kitur's mum said to Ben, though her eyes were cold and hard. She breathed deeply through her nose a few times. "But I am very disappointed in you, Kitur. If you hadn't broken the rules none of this would have happened."

Kitur looked down at his shoes as the lift slowed to a stop.

"I'm going to confiscate your Virtual Reality console for an entire month," his mum said.

The doors opened before Kitur could respond. His parents stepped out of the lift and walked towards the car.

"Thanks for coming clean, Ben," Kitur whispered, as they followed behind his parents. "You're a good friend."

Ben bit his bottom lip and clasped his hands together. He didn't exactly feel like a good friend. He was just glad that he'd got his body back. And Kitur's father still had a job.

"You'll have to come over to my house again sometime," Kitur continued. "Maybe next weekend?"

"I'd love to," Ben said. And he really meant it. Kitur was actually all right. And it wasn't like either of them had loads of other friends. "But I might wait until you get your VR console back!"

STORY SEVEN

My little sister Ruby is *so* cute. When you tickle her she giggles like an angel and gets these lovely dimples on each cheek.

Her tickliest spots are under her chin and on the tip of her nose. So I thought it would be funny to tickle her nose with a feather, but it wasn't funny. It was a nightmare!

She was sitting on my chest with her little legs dangling down over my shoulders. She can't really sit up on her own too well, so I had to grip her waist, which made it pretty difficult to tickle her. So I clenched the feather between my teeth and tickled her nose with it. It was one of those big pink feathers that can't have come from a real bird. Anyway, I was holding onto her, with the feather poking out my mouth. She was giggling away, her little dimples practically glowing, when I felt a sneeze coming along.

Have you ever tried to sneeze with something poking out of your mouth? It's pretty difficult. For a second I was worried the feather would shoot out like an arrow and spear my sister in the eye. Just as the sneeze hit I saw that Ruby was sneezing too. She's even cuter when she sneezes than when she giggles. Anyway, the funny thing was that we both sneezed at *exactly* the same time. Right in each other's faces. Except that it wasn't funny at all!

We sneezed. And when I opened my eyes I was staring at my own face. At first I couldn't figure out what was going on. Was I looking in a mirror? Then I saw a big smile appear on my features.

"Baba!" I said, sounding exactly like a baby.

It took a few seconds before I figured out what had happened. I was in my baby sister's body, sitting on my own chest. Ruby was in my body and she clearly didn't know how to drive it properly. Her arms flopped around at her sides and she was wriggling so much that I felt like a cowboy riding a bucking bronco. I quickly threw my arms out for balance, swung my legs over and hopped off myself.

This was weird.

It was really, *really* weird.

"Ruby?" I said, leaning over my ten-year-old body and looking right into my face. "Are you okay?"

"Baba!" she said. "Oooby!" That's how she says her own name.

"Yes … this is Ruby's body. But inside is me … Emily."

"Milly?"

The poor little thing. She didn't know what was going on. Neither did I, for that matter. Not really. All I knew was that I did not want to stay trapped in my sister's one-year-old body. It's hard enough to fit in at school in a regular-sized body. It would be impossible looking like that.

I picked up the pink feather that was lying on the floor. We must have swapped bodies by sneezing at the same time, so surely we'd swap back if we did it again.

"Stay still, Ruby," I said, climbing back onto her chest and sticking the feather in my mouth. It was way harder to hold it this time. Ruby only had her bottom front teeth so the feather kept pointing upwards, tickling my own nose and making me sneeze. When I finally managed to point it forwards and tickle Ruby on my nose she only giggled. No dimples this time. And no sneezes.

What were we going to do?

Just at that moment Mum called from the kitchen. "Emily … Ruby … Breakfast time!"

Oh no! What was I going to tell Mum? She was going to have a heart attack. I jumped off my chest and tried to roll my big little sister over, but she was way bigger than me now. I was going to need Mum's help.

I left Ruby lying on the sitting-room floor in my body and walked into the kitchen.

"Ruby? You're walking!" said Mum, blinking rapidly. "I can't believe it!"

"Try not to panic, Mum!" I said, holding Ruby's little hands out, palms facing forwards.

Mum dropped the carton of milk she was holding and it made a loud thud, spilling a white puddle onto the floor. She raised her hands to her mouth and stared at me wide-eyed.

I was tempted to have a bit of fun and do a cartwheel across the middle of the kitchen, but I needed Mum's help. She wouldn't be much use if she had to be rushed to A&E due to heart failure.

"I know this looks weird," I said quickly, my voice all squeaky and high-pitched. "But Ruby and I have just had an accident. I was tickling her nose with a feather when we both sneezed at the same time."

Mum stared at me blankly. She reached out and steadied herself on the counter.

"We swapped bodies, Mum," I said. "This is me, Emily, and Ruby is in the living room in my body."

"But … but …" said Mum, who is very rarely lost for words. "… that's impossible!"

"Yeah, it's pretty crazy all right," I said. "You've gotta help us get back to normal, Mum."

She nodded, even though her mouth was still wide open. Then she moved towards me, stepping right in the puddle of milk and making big white footprints on the floor. Perhaps Mum

wasn't going to be much help after all. Adults aren't great in crazy situations. I think they've spent so long being normal that their brains just can't handle it. Kids, on the other hand, are usually fine.

"Hi, Ruby," I said, once we'd arrived in the living room.

She was lying on her back with her hands in front of her face, wiggling her fingers and smiling at them. It was funny how she could still be cute, even in my ten-year-old body. I gave her a quick tickle under the chin and she giggled.

Mum was still struggling to find any words. "Hi ... darling ..." she said eventually, although she sounded about as warm as a snowman's butt. "We'll get you, errrm, back to normal soon."

"Let's go and have some breakfast," I said, hoping that she might be able to focus better if Ruby was occupied with some food. It took ages for Mum to lift my body up and carry it into the kitchen. Ruby was giggling, thinking

it was a game. All I could do in this little body was offer a few words of encouragement.

When Mum arrived at the dining table she stopped and stared at the seating with her eyebrows squished together. "How's this going to work?" she asked.

There was no way my body was going to fit in the high chair but Ruby didn't yet have the balance for a normal chair. And we couldn't exactly put her breakfast bowl on the floor like she was a dog.

"I know," I said, "why don't you stick her in one of the normal chairs, then hook my T-shirt over the back. That should keep her upright."

Mum grunted as she lifted my body up again and plopped it into the chair. She held it steady with her left hand, while lifting my T-shirt up and over the wooden chair. It made Ruby – or me – look a bit like a hunchback but it kept my body upright enough for now.

While Mum went off to get a bowl of cereal I looked up at the high chair, trying to work out the best way to get into it. After all, Ruby's

body was pretty tiny and high chairs are called high chairs for a good reason. I was never going to be able to climb up the chair itself, so I pulled myself up onto a normal chair, and then hopped onto the table.

"Baba funny!" said Ruby, giggling as I carefully dodged the vase of flowers in the middle of the table. Once I got to the high chair I stepped over the tray and plopped myself down in the seat. It was actually quite comfortable, especially because my bottom was nicely padded in a nappy. And thankfully I'd changed Ruby just before we switched, so I didn't have to sit in Ruby's wee.

Mum was staring at me from the other side of the kitchen with her mouth hanging open like a fly trap. She shook her head slightly, then said, "Do you know where the milk is?"

I smiled and pointed at the white puddle on the floor.

"Oh dear," Mum said, then she picked the carton up, gave it a shake, and poured the remains over some Weet-Bix for Ruby. It wasn't like Mum to not care about a milk spillage, but I suppose we did have a much bigger mess that needed cleaning up first.

"So, what's the plan, Mum?" I asked. She was the adult, surely she would be able to come up with something.

"We should probably go and see the doctor," said Mum, plopping herself down in the chair opposite me.

Oh, great. Why do adults think that doctors can solve everything? Knowing Dr Greene, he'd just say that we've got a virus and prescribe us some antibiotics.

"I think we should try to sort this out ourselves first," I said. "All we need to do is get us both to sneeze at exactly the same

time, right in each other's faces. If it worked once, surely it will work again."

"I guess it's worth a try," Mum said, brushing a strand of hair from in front of her eye. "But if you're not back to normal by lunchtime I'm booking you in to the doctor's."

I glanced up at my own body. Ruby was busily scooping up Weet-Bix with my fingers and there was more of it on my face than in my mouth. I really didn't fancy sitting in the doctor's waiting room for hours with Ruby looking like that. We had to sort this out ourselves.

"So … what things make you sneeze?" I asked. "Tickling with a feather, obviously. Only it didn't work so well when I tried it a second time."

"I often sneeze when I look at the sun," Mum said, and we both glanced at the rain trickling down the windowpane. It was so dark out that it looked more like late evening than nine o'clock on a Saturday morning. "But that's not going to help us today, is it?"

"No, and neither would hay fever."

"Plucking nose hair often makes me sneeze too," Mum added with a laugh. I tilted my head back and squished Ruby's nose up to show that one-year-olds don't have nose hair. It was good to see Mum relaxing a little, though.

"How about fizzy drinks?" I said. "They sometimes make me sneeze."

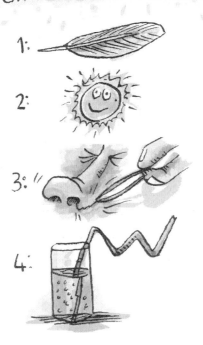

SNEEZE MAKING THINGS

1:

2:

3:

4:

Mum raised her eyebrows and nodded before going to look in the fridge. She came back a moment later with some lemonade, a cup and a beaker. She poured a bit of lemonade into each, then passed the beaker to me.

I looked up at her and smiled without taking it.

"Sorry, love," Mum said. "Force of habit."

Once Ruby had the beaker I quickly took a sip of lemonade and peered right into my own face. It was so weird seeing myself from the outside like this. My eyes seemed bluer than normal and I looked younger than I usually feel, but perhaps that was due to the one-year-old expressions that kept lighting up my face.

Ruby took a swig from the beaker and my eyes widened. Instead of a sneeze Ruby snorted, spraying lemonade out of her nose and right into my face. Even with liquid dripping from the end of both of our noses neither of us could manage a sneeze.

We needed a better idea.

Then it hit me.

"Sneezing powder!" I said loudly. "One time Matiu Taylor bought a packet of sneezing powder to school and it was amazing. It had the whole class sneezing within seconds!"

"But where can we get sneezing power?" Mum asked.

"In the joke shop in town," I said. "They've got everything in there."

"And you want to walk into town?"

No, that was pretty much the last thing I wanted to do. It was raining, for starters. And what if someone from school saw us? They'd think I'd gone completely bonkers. But the doctor's surgery was the only alternative and I didn't like the sound of that either.

"Not really," I said, "but what choice do we have? Nothing else seems to be working!"

Leaving home is always a bit of a nightmare with a baby. It takes ages to get all their clothes on, get them in the pram. Grab spare nappies. All of that stuff. Now imagine what it's like with a ten-year-old baby!

At first Mum just grabbed the usual nappies. "Mum," I said, shaking my head. "If I need the toilet I'll tell you. We need a nappy that will fit a ten-year-old!"

In the end we had to wrap a hand towel around her and then put her trousers over the top. Then we had to try to squeeze her into the pram, which wasn't easy.

It was about twenty minutes before we even left the house. And when we did we weren't exactly inconspicuous. Mum looked wide-eyed and flustered. The ten-year-old was crammed into a small pram and the one-year-old was running along next to the pram, trying desperately to keep up.

The problem was that Ruby's legs just didn't have any muscles in them. And her woollen shoes were hopeless. They got soaking wet and I could feel every stone. We'd barely reached

the end of the road before Mum had to pick me up.

Poor Mum. It wasn't easy pushing the pram and carrying me at the same time, even though I could help her by holding the umbrella. And I think the rain might actually have been a good thing. It meant that there were fewer people around to see us. Plus Mum had put the rain screen up on the pram, so if we did bump into someone we knew there was a chance they wouldn't see my sister babbling away in my body.

When we got to the joke shop my little heart did a triple somersault. The shop was packed with kids of all ages, probably looking for something fun to do on a rainy day. What if there was someone I knew in there?

"Just leave us out here, Mum," I said, desperate to avoid bumping into a classmate.

"It's raining," Mum said. "And besides, I can't leave a one-year-old outside a shop. You're not a dog!"

She put me down on the pavement and unzipped the rain cover before wheeling the pram into the shop. I kept hold of the umbrella and tried to position it so that it covered both me and the pram.

"Would you put that down inside, please dear," Mum said. "It's bad luck!"

What was she like? It certainly wasn't as bad luck as being spotted picking your nose or peeing your pants by someone in your class. And anyway, I had just accidentally swapped bodies with my one-year-old sister – how much worse could my luck actually get?

Just as I had that thought, two girls from my class, Tenecia and Madeline, walked into the shop.

I nearly died, right there and then.

Tenecia's a good friend and has been over to my house heaps. But Madeline and I don't see eye to eye at all, even when we're the same height. She always bosses me around and tells me what to do. And she says mean things about people behind their backs. I didn't want to think about what she'd say if she saw me sitting in a pram picking my nose.

"Hi, Mrs Harman!" said Tenecia, instantly spotting my mum. "Where's Emily today?"

My mum's mouth dropped open and her face reddened. "Hi, Tenecia, fancy seeing you here!" Mum said, glancing down at the pram. Fortunately, it was pointing away from the door or I would have been spotted already. I needed to think fast.

"Tinny!" I said, trying to sound like a baby. "Hi, Tinny!"

Tenecia turned towards me, her face lit up like a beacon. "Ruby knows my name!" she said loudly. "And she's walking. That is so amazing."

Madeline bent down beside me and put on her biggest, smiliest baby face.

"Whooooshie, boooooshie, Wuuuubie," she said, speaking in that ridiculous tone that so many people use on babies. "Can you say 'Madeline'? Mah-duh-lin."

I couldn't help myself at this point. Baby-talk is one of my pet hates. And I was a bit annoyed that Tenecia had chosen to hang out with Madeline today rather than me.

"Yes, I can," I said perfectly clearly. "But I thought it was Madeline, not Ma-blur-blin!" I copied her stupid baby-speak as well as I could.

Madeline's mouth dropped open, giving her a baffled-goldfish look. "Wow!" she muttered, in normal-human English. "That's incredible."

"How long has Ruby been talking for?" Tenecia asked. "Emily never told me!"

I left Mum to do the talking and toddled over to the shelf with all the powders and fake poos. I tried to walk like a one-year-old, to avoid Mum having to answer any more difficult questions. There was only one packet of sneezing powder left, but that stuff was so strong one would definitely be enough. The problem was that it was halfway up the shelf, just out of reach of my short arms.

"Over here, Mum," I said, once Tenecia and Madeline had gone off to look at the wigs and rubber masks. "There it is!"

Mum came over and went to grab the packet I was pointing to. But she'd left the pram in the middle of the shop and Ruby didn't like that one bit.

Before Mum was able to get the sneezing powder, Ruby went into one of her meltdowns.

She is super-cute, my sister. But she can also be super-loud. And when she gets started it's very difficult to stop her without giving her a lolly to suck or a smartphone to play on. Mum rushed over to soothe her, but I could see Tenecia, Madeline and everyone else in the shop craning their necks to see what was going on.

This was an absolute nightmare and Mum didn't even seem to care what people thought. "Calm down, Ruby," she was saying, almost loud enough for everyone to hear.

I rushed over. One of us had to take control of the situation.

"Just give her your cell phone and take her outside!" I said sternly. "I'll get the sneezing powder, if you give me the money to pay for it."

Fortunately, Mum didn't argue with me. It's funny though, because I'd never get away with talking to her like that in my own body.

The crying stopped as soon as Ruby got her hands on the phone, and once Mum had zipped up the rain cover there was less chance that anyone would see that it was me having the meltdown. Then she handed me a twenty-dollar note and went outside, leaving me on my own in the shop in Ruby's tiny body.

I had to figure out a way to reach the last packet of sneezing powder before someone else did. I was still holding the folded-down umbrella, which was taller than I was, so perhaps I'd be able to use that to knock it off the shelf. Clutching the pointy end in my hand I held it up and tried to hook the packet with the handle. At first I just hooked onto the plastic shelf, then when I did get it over the packet the thing just folded it in half, making it impossible to knock off. This wasn't going to work. I needed something to stand on so that I could grab it with my hands.

There was a small stepladder on the other side of the shop, so I weaved between a few pairs of legs to get to it. It was funny how tall everyone looked from so low down. Even kids my age looked like giants. When I got to the stepladder I gripped it on each side and pushed it along the floor as though using it to keep balance. The feet made a deep vibrating sound, like a trombone, as they scraped along the floor.

"Awww, isn't she cute!" someone said from behind me, but I kept moving forwards, my eyes focused on the sneezing powder.

I was nearly there, only a few metres to go, when Tinny and Madeline walked up to the shelf, their backs towards me.

"Look, they've got one pack of sneezing powder left!" Tinny said, pointing at the folded-over packet.

"I'm gonna get it and sprinkle some on my brother's pillow," Madeline said with a smirk.

I watched in horror as Madeline plucked the packet off the shelf and turned towards the counter. The last thing I wanted was for them to see me – or my baby sister – standing alone in the middle of the joke shop. I quickly dashed over towards the costume rack and slipped between a big furry lion and a Batman costume. All I could do was watch helplessly as Madeline paid for the sneezing powder and Tenecia bought a purple wig. They then turned and strolled towards the door, dodging the stepladder that was still in the middle of the shop floor.

This was an absolute disaster. There was no more sneezing powder left in the shop and my friends were now on their way outside, where my own body was sat in a pram, probably gurgling away like a baby. I rushed towards the door but it closed in my face. All I could do was watch them through the glass. It had stopped raining and there were more people out on the street now. Mum stood in the middle of the sidewalk, one hand on the pram's handle and the other impatiently pulling at a strand of hair.

"Hi, Mrs Harman," Madeline said, full of politeness and smiles, which is how she always acts when there are adults around. Then she looked down at the pair of trainers poking out below the pram cover and her face dropped. "Is that Emily in the pram?" she asked, her voice high-pitched and her eyebrows squished together.

Mum's eyes bulged and all her muscles went tense. "Errr … yes. She's not feeling very well today! It's best if we leave her alone."

But Madeline wasn't listening, like always. It felt like my lungs were filled with water as she leaned over and pulled the cover up.

Ruby looked up from the phone, her mouth open and her eyes wide with surprise. This would have been totally fine in her own body but it made me look completely bonkers.

"Goo goo!" she said loudly, and Madeline and Tenecia both stepped back, letting out long fake laughs, as though I was playing a trick on them.

I had to do something before this situation got any worse.

At that moment someone arrived at the shop, obscuring my view. They pulled the door open and I slipped out through the gap, carefully dodging their legs. Tenecia and Madeline were still standing in the middle of the pavement, completely speechless, and I spotted the sneezing powder poking out of Madeline's back pocket.

That was the only thing that could fix this crazy mess, so I rushed towards Madeline's bottom. I reached up with my little hand and grabbed hold of the corner of the packet. Madeline spun around and looked down at me – or Ruby – standing in the middle of the pavement, the sneezing powder in my hand.

"No, Wuby," she said in her best baby voice. "Mine!"

Her hand shot forwards and she grabbed hold of the other end of the packet and tried to yank it from my grip. But there was no way I was going to let it go. I just had to get back into my own body before Ruby did anything else embarrassing. I held on with both hands and pulled as hard as my little arms could manage.

There was a tearing sound and I landed on my bottom on the pavement, half a packet still clenched in my fingers. A cloud of powder filled the air, engulfing my mum, the pram and anyone else who happened to be on the street.

Everyone started sneezing instantly.

Mum.

Madeline.

Tenecia.

Ruby in my body.

Me in Ruby's body.

Even strangers in the street.

There were sneezes of all shapes and sizes.

I sneezed four times straight and when I'd finished, tears filled my eyes. But they were nothing to do with the sneezing. I had failed. The packet was now in two empty halves and I couldn't think of any other way to get back into my own body.

Most people had stopped sneezing and were busy rubbing their eyes and wiping their noses. I looked up at Ruby, sitting in the pram in my body. She did one final sneeze, then the edges of her mouth curled upwards and her eyes squinted.

She looked like she was doing a wee.

SHE WAS DOING A WEE!

I stared on in horror as a damp patch appeared on my jeans and began to spread, the hand-towel nappy clearly not doing its job. I had to do something before anybody saw me.

I pushed myself up off the ground and ran towards the pram. When I was close enough I took a flying leap straight onto my own lap, covering up the wet patch. I was going so fast that our heads donked and Ruby let out a yelp.

"It's okay, Ruby!" I whispered right into her face, as I reached up and pulled the cover down over us.

I felt something trickle down from the top of the cover and watched as my own nose twitched right in front of my eyes.

Aahh AAHH, choo, CHOO! Achoo, ACHOO, AAAACHOOOO!

We both sneezed three times each.

When I'd finished sneezing there was a nasty damp feeling between my legs. Ruby's cute little face was staring down at me, all smile and dimples.

"Milly!" she said, and I hugged her really tightly. Partly because I loved her so much and was extremely happy that we were both back in our own bodies. And partly because she was covering up the wet patch.

"Bless you, Ruby!" I whispered, then I moved my head to the side, just in case we both sneezed again.

"What's up with you guys today?" Tenecia asked, and I suddenly noticed that she, Madeline and my mother were staring at us through the plastic window of the rain cover.

I flipped the cover up and put on a casual smile.

"Oh, we're all right," I said. "But Ruby just hasn't been feeling herself."

"I can't believe she stole my sneezing powder!" Madeline said, rubbing one of her eyebrows.

"Sorry about that, Maddy," I said, and I really was. Perhaps she wasn't all that bad. "We'll buy you another packet when they get more in. And I'll see you both in school on Monday."

Mum didn't pick up the hint at all. She just let out a long puff of breath, the palm of her hand covering her heart.

"I think we'd better get home and let Ruby have a nap," I said loudly.

Mum nodded and started to push the pram with both of us in it. She looked like she needed a nap too. And I *really* needed to change my pants!

About the Author

Tom E. Moffatt wouldn't switch lives with anyone else, even if he had his own mind-swapping machine. He lives in beautiful New Zealand with his loving wife, three gorgeous daughters and a very tolerant cat called Nina. And he gets to spend his time transforming words into laughter. However, if he did get caught up in a mind-swapping muddle, he would want to become a duck. Ducks are awesome. They get to fly, walk and float, and they skip winter by migrating to warmer climates. He would, however, try to avoid duck-hunting season, if at all possible.

For more silliness, jokes and information go to
www.TomEMoffatt.com

Acknowledgements

Huge thanks to Rotorua Civic Arts Trust for their generous financial support towards this book. Thanks to Paul Beavis, for making my stories come to life with his incredible illustrations. Anna Bowles for her insightful and meticulous editing. Marj Griffiths for proofreading and Valentina Dordevic for her blurb writing skills. Smartwork Creative for their design prowess. Peter Williams for his hunting stories and tips.

Thanks to all my Guinea pig readers at Otonga School and beyond: Oscar Burns, Isla Osborne, Callum Duncan Temple-Doig, Keely, Ella Scott, Sophie Patterson, Amani Sinisa, Lia Sinisa, Charis Whiteman & Alastair Rogers.

Thanks to Snobes: my wife, chief Guinea pig, critique partner, editor, motivator and guidance counsellor.

Finally, thanks to you – the reader – for giving this book a go and for getting all the way to the end.

24984746R00144

Printed in Great Britain
by Amazon